BARRY C

Endangered
Species

THE CRIME CLUB
An Imprint of HarperCollins *Publishers*

First published in Great Britain in 1992
by The Crime Club, an imprint of
HarperCollins Publishers, 77–85 Fulham Palace Road,
Hammersmith, London W6 8JB

9 8 7 6 5 4 3 2 1

Barry Cork asserts the moral right to be identified
as the author of this work.

A catalogue record for this book is
available from the British Library

ISBN 0 00 232421 0

Photoset in Linotron Baskerville by
Rowland Phototypesetting Ltd
Bury St Edmunds, Suffolk
Printed and bound in Great Britain by
HarperCollins Book Manufacturing, Glasgow

For
My Wife,
a very knowledgeable non-playing member

There was never a Wendal Fen airfield, and no 901 Squadron ever served in the Eighth Air Force. It is happily true that veterans from the United States of America still make their individual pilgrimages to the sites of airfields that were known to them half a century ago. Many of these are helped in their researches by the Second Air Division Memorial Trust, and its Memorial Room in Norwich has become a meeting place for one time air crew. However, so far as I have been able to discover there is no such organisation as the Allied Air Veterans' Association based on Cambridge or anywhere else, and its function and personnel are wholly fiction.

B.C.

CHAPTER 1

I filled up near Wisbech and the man asked if there was anything else I needed because garages weren't all that plentiful the way I was going.

'Snow tyres?' I suggested. It was the first week in October.

'You won't larf if you break down.'

The chap at the pump was inspecting the Maserati trident insignia on the front of the car. 'Italian job, innit?'

'Yes,' I said. 'And I don't intend breaking down.'

One says these things, unthinking little challenges to Them. Sometimes one gets away with it. Sometimes not. But don't ever think they're not noted. Because they most certainly are.

West of the Wash the land is flat as your hand. In winter the winds are said to blow uninterrupted from the North Pole and the chill factor makes a stranger think of the rest of England as subtropical. The men who farm these parts plant *Cuppressus leylandii* four square around their houses like walls, so that there is at least something to act as a windbreak, and you can see this house and the next and the one after that dumped down like odd little geometric copses a few miles apart amid the hedgeless fields of black soil that stretch for ever beneath the huge cloudless sky.

Fen country. Not everybody's country. Not mine, come to think of it, but at least if you were dropped down on it by parachute you'd know you weren't in Purley or Pinner. God knows how many thousands of years ago this had been part of the North Sea, a vast bay bitten into by the eastern coastline that extended from Lincolnshire in the north to Cambridgeshire in the south. The bay had eventually silted up, forming a lake of no mean size. People have been kept busy draining the area ever since.

We drove for what seemed a long time. From behind me, eight-year-old Sam said, 'Funny kind of place.'

'Yes.'

'The roads are jolly straight.'

Well, yes. Empty, too. Small son speaks with forked tongue, conjuring question of what a Maserati Khamsin will do anyway. A hundred and thirty? Forty? Forget you're a policeman, man, and burn a little rubber.

Laurie, at my side, said, 'Angus, don't be a fool!'

'Och, lassie, just a wee squirt.' I selected first, ran the motor up to two thousand revs and let her go. Pretty restrained stuff but satisfying. Eight cylinders, four cam-shafts, miles of timing chain. God knows how many valves suddenly thrashing around creates a mesmeric sound if you like that sort of thing. The Khamsin was no small car but it squatted down for an instant on its fat back wheels and then fairly leapt. I watched the needle of the rev counter swing in a fast steady arc as the rubber bit on the road. 4000. 4500. 5000. I yanked the gear-shift back to second and there was a high crack like a small bore pistol, and I was holding the chrome-plated lever loose in my hand.

Sam's reproachful voice was behind my left ear, like my conscience. 'You told me I wasn't to say that.'

I apologized, but my heart wasn't in it. There can be few things more frustrating than sitting behind 6 litres of superlative engine with the knowledge that for the foresee-able future one is locked in second gear. I looked at the fair-haired girl beside me. 'And don't laugh.'

'I wasn't going to laugh.'

It was hard to tell one way or the other because her eyes were covered by big sunglasses, their lenses darkened by the low sun. Would I have been able to tell anyway? Probably not. Laurie Wilson was my literary agent, Sam's good friend and, since my divorce from Angela, the woman in my life. I wondered how well I knew this loving friend. Not very well, perhaps. Not her, nor any woman.

I said, 'Come to think of it, it's no laughing matter. Nobody in their right mind wants to break down in the Fens.'

'The garage chap warned you.'

'I know.' I was back at about thirty miles an hour now, coasting along up an almost unnoticeable rise, the kind of thing you'd feel on a bicycle but hardly in a car. There was a sort of bulge in the road that looked as though it might do service as a lay-by, so I drove into it, switched off and got out.

'It's *creepy!*' Since the divorce, a largely urban child, but Sam came and stood beside me and his small paw found my hand in search of reassurance at the sight of so much space. Then: 'Do you suppose that's a river or a waterway?' Waterway was something of a new word.

I said, 'I think it's something they call a drain.'

'It's awfully big for a drain.'

'Well,' I told him, 'it drains the water off rather a lot of land.' But as Sam said, it was a big drain. More like a canal. It ran straight as an arrow as far as the eye could see, and the road we were on ran beside it. No trees, no signposts. It was summer, but the wind moaned steadily out of the pale vault of a huge sky. I told myself that Peterborough couldn't have been more than forty miles away, King's Lynn even less, but it didn't make any difference, because to all intents and purposes this was the end of the world. I felt a sense of personal unease, as though I'd turned up somewhere uninvited.

Easy to be over-imaginative. We got back in the car with Laurie. 'There's some kind of building a mile or so ahead,' I told her. 'Maybe there's even a phone.'

'What kind of building? A house?'

I said, 'No, bigger than that. Some kind of barn. It looks a bit like an old aircraft hangar.'

'Could be the remains of another World War Two air-field. There seem to have been dozens of them.' Laurie bent over the map on her lap. 'Nothing marked here except something tiny called Wendal. The whole of this place seems to be Wendal Fen.'

'Well, there's no point in hanging about here.' I started the car and we proceeded in a stately fashion appropriate to second gear. In point of fact, a Maserati Khamsin will go quite fast in second with the engine turning over at some astronomic number of revs, but I'm all for a quiet life. After about a mile it was possible to see our goal quite clearly. It had been a hangar all right. Most of the land round it was cultivated but there were still traces of concrete dispersal bays, nameless unidentifiable lumps of building block and rusting sheet iron.

Coming towards us along what must once have been the perimeter track a Land-Rover took shape, slowed as it came abreast and then stopped.

'You in trouble or do you usually drive that slow?' The head leaning out of the window was a comic-strip portrait of a middle-aged Viking, all fair hair and bright blue, slightly mad eyes. No wonder the locals made themselves scarce when a few boatloads of Norsemen arrived. Even today, this one looked as though he might still take his rape and pillage seriously.

I held up my gear lever for his inspection.

'Ah!' My Norseman came down from his Land-Rover, a huge man, walking delicately, as heavy people often do. He was wearing a Barbour jacket, with cord trousers tucked into rubber boots, and the hand that reached out for my offering looked like something attached to a JCB. He ran a thumb over the broken end. 'Stress fracture?'

'Or a freak flaw.' I was defensive about the marque Maserati, my pride and joy. In point of fact, Italian engineering genius had been ofttimes let down by inferior materials, but so far as I was concerned, such troubles had been confined to lesser cars. I said, 'It's going to be difficult to weld, with the break that low down.'

'Easier to have a new one made up.'

Well, yes. Whatever local garage there was would know more about tractors than exotic Italian sports cars, but the man was only trying to help. I asked, 'Do you happen to know a good man?'

'I do, as a matter of fact.' The Viking nodded towards the ancient hangar. 'The fellow who rents that place from me. Pat Smith. Lunatic who spends all his time and money fooling around with old aircraft. But give the devil his due. Good with his hands.' He climbed back behind the wheel of the Land-Rover. 'My name's Hayward, by the way. Saul Hayward.'

'Angus Straun.'

He looked hard at me. 'A Scot.'

I nodded. With a name like mine, what else?

'Hah!' I saw his eyes change. 'We killed your king at Flodden.'

Well, we all have our own small talk, and writing historical novels as a hobby has to pay off some time. Flodden Field, battle of. My memory bank came up with 1513 or thereabouts. Attempted invasion of England by King James IV of Scotland. And yes, James got the chop. I said, 'Aye. He was a bonny lad, too, by all accounts.'

Hayward glared. 'Dēað bið sēlla eorla gehwylcum þonne edwīt-líf!'

I recognized the quotation. *Beowulf.* I said, 'Better a noble death than a life of shame.' In my undergraduate days I'd often wondered when I'd find a use for Anglo-Saxon. Now I knew. Hayward grunted and let up the clutch. I got back in the Maserati and followed the Land-Rover through a sea of sugar beet, that most unromantic of crops.

'And what,' Laurie asked, 'was the Beowulf bit about?'

'I'm waiting to find out myself,' I told her. 'Keep in touch.'

There was more left of Wendal Fen airfield than I'd expected. At the end of World War Two East Anglia was a vast patchwork of airfields from which the Allies had launched their bombers against Germany. Most of them had been built on land requisitioned from local farmers, and with the ending of hostilities they were handed back. Digging up concrete runways can't have been easy, but over the years most of them disappeared. A few remained, usually because the owner wanted to build hen batteries on good hard standing. Here at Wendal there was still a perimeter track and at least a part of the original runway, weedy but serviceable, stretching out between the crops.

'Gosh! This was really an airfield?' Sam's practical experience was limited to the Terminals at London Airport but he had a small boy's enthusiasm for comic-strip air warfare. He said, 'They had Spitfires here?'

I shook my head. 'I don't think so. All bombers.'

'How do you know?' The first burgeoning doubts of a parent's infallibility. I thought wryly that last year my word would have been gospel.

'They were all bomber stations in these parts. Fighters didn't have enough range to cross to Europe over the North Sea.' I didn't really know but it seemed like a reprise of something I must have read somewhere. I caught Laurie's eye and detected a certain scepticism, but then that could have been there anyway. The hangar was looming up ahead, larger than I'd expected. The Land-Rover stopped beside a youngish man in blue overalls who was unloading packing cases from a jeep. Patrick Smith. We unloaded ourselves and Hayward explained our troubles, briefly, accurately, no mistakes over names.

'We can turn you up a new shaft, no problem.' Smith glanced at what was left of the Khamsin's gear lever before handing it back. I judged him to be in his middle thirties, a controlled, capable character with an expensive voice and dark good looks that would have photographed well if he'd been that way inclined. Like Hayward, he fingered the fracture of the metal. 'I suspect some cowboy garage hand has been let loose on your car at some time or other—bits like this should last for ever. Maybe we'd better have a look at the linkage while we're at it.'

'It's very good of you,' I said, and meant it.

He looked at me as though a bit surprised I could speak. 'That's all right.' He sounded perfectly friendly but it would have helped my conscience if he'd smiled and I got the impression that he didn't want us there but he couldn't actually bring himself to tell us to go away. We stood there in the pale summer sunshine, with that everlasting wind stirring the dust off the old concrete, your classic grouping of typical Englishmen all bent on doing the right thing.

I had sudden misgivings. 'Look,' I said, 'there's no reason for us to hold you up. If you'd tell us where the nearest garage is . . .'

Unexpectedly Smith smiled. Rather engagingly, as though it was something he'd just remembered how to do. 'My dear chap, you don't know the local garage. Besides, we like making bits and pieces. I'll get this place opened up and then you can drive inside so we can get a proper look at your gearbox.'

Hayward watched him go away. 'It's true,' he said, 'they're good at that sort of thing.'

'They?'

'He's got two or three helpers.'

The helpers were presumably working inside because

after a couple of minutes the hangar doors rolled open
enough to let in a car, so I got back behind the wheel of
the Khamsin and drove through.

And Sam said, 'Wow!'

It was easy for him because he was small and could see
out of the car and up, but so far as I was concerned I'd
driven from brilliant daylight into shadow. Odd, because
looking ahead through the windscreen I could see that the
hangar was ablaze with lights. So why was I in the dark?
I switched off and got out, the better to find out. Not that
it was difficult. As soon as my feet touched the floor I
realized why we were in shadow.

I'd parked the car under the wing of an enormous aircraft.

I suppose today's intercontinental jets are so big that
one expects fifty-year-old warplanes to be tiny, pathetic
achievements of an earlier age. Maybe the bodies weren't
all that big but the wingspan that supported each bomb-
laden fuselage was enormous. I stood and stared upwards,
taking in the two massive radial engines set in the wing
above me, the great, boat-shaped body built up of polished
aluminium, twin rudders like sails.

Smith looked down at Sam. 'Know what it is, son?'

'A B-24!' He didn't spend sizeable amounts of pocket
money on plastic models for nothing. 'We called them
Liberators.'

'Made by?'

'Consolidated Aircraft.' Sam added for good measure,
'The engines are Pratt and Whitney Twin Wasps. 1200
horsepower. Bomb load 8000 pounds. Range 3000 miles.' I
could have done as much for a Le Mans Bentley at his age.
I tried not to be impressed.

Smith smiled faintly. 'Range depends on the load, but
not bad. This is a B-24D actually. The RAF called it a
Mark IV.'

'Did you fly it in the war?'

'I'm afraid not.' Smith wouldn't have been born until about the middle 1950s but he didn't comment on the fact. I suspected he had a Sam or two of his own somewhere. He went on, 'I sort of rescued it from the scrap heap. My friends and I have been rebuilding it for the last couple of years.'

Sam said breathlessly, 'I think that's super! Is she ready to fly again now?'

'I've test flown her. She's good as new. A bit better, probably, in some respects.' Smith turned Sam round to me and gave him a shove. 'Now you wait with your Dad while we have a look at his car. Another time I'll show you over the plane. OK?'

'Yes, of course! OK!' Sam glowed, eyes full of eight-year-old hero worship. I resisted the impulse to give him a fatherly pat because fathers were at a discount today. Instead I went to where Hayward and Laurie had made themselves comfortable on a couple of packing cases. I asked him if he had taken a hand in the restoration of the old bomber.

'By the gods, no! A simple Saxon yeoman, that's me. Not that it's all that simple these days.' Those rather wild blue eyes studied me. 'And you, Straun. What's your business?'

I studied him back, not meeting an Anglo-Saxon-speaking yeoman who swore by the old gods every day of the week.

'I'm a policeman,' I said finally. These days people aren't in the habit of running screaming from the room at the news but I always felt it was a kind of admission. The honest copper, we were told as children, is everyone's friend. Patently not true. Maybe getting even less true the shiftier society becomes. But what the hell. If you prick us, do we not bleed?

Hayward stared at me curiously, as though searching for undetected horns. 'The devil you are!' He paused. 'The writer, Angus Straun. The *Blood Debt* chap. Read some-where that he's a policeman in his spare time.'

Enormously gratifying suddenly to become someone who fiddled about being a policeman in his spare time. I said, 'I suppose that about sums me up. But yes, *Blood Debt* was one of mine.' I didn't look at Laurie, who shared this engaging heresy that I was a writer first and foremost. Could it be she was right after all?

Hayward said vehemently, 'In my opinion you are a splendid historical writer. Plenty of blood, the way it was. Hope they reward you well.'

Nobody had called me a splendid writer to my face before and I rather liked it. Possibly an admiring public palls if one has too much of it but historical novels as a genre rarely arouse extravagant emotions. 'I don't know about the rewards,' I told him. 'You'd better ask Miss Wilson about them. She's my agent.'

'Is she now?' Hayward studied Laurie as though he were seeing her for the first time. Which perhaps he was. I had already formed the impression that he was no feminist, but apparently he made exceptions.

Laurie said, 'Yes,' in the rather flat voice she uses to indicate that if you're bent on trouble she's fully prepared to dish it out.

'I'm sure you are mutually fortunate.' Hayward looked back at me. 'My dear fellow, I don't want to appear inquisi-tive, but are you working on anything at the moment?'

'Well—yes.'

'The same period as *Blood Debt*?'

I don't really like talking about my books, still less when I'm still writing them, but admirers get under one's skin. And what writer won't stand on his head for a spot of publicity or a good review? 'No,' I said, 'not exactly. *Blood Debt* was mediæval. This one's set a bit earlier. About Hereward.'

'The Wake? How very extraordinary!'

Well, he must have been an extraordinary character, Hereward, the Saxon who'd continued to fight William of Normandy long after the rest of his countrymen had forsaken the memory of Harold and sworn allegiance to a foreign king. A thousand years ago Hereward had taken refuge in the fens, in those days even less hospitable than they were now. He'd fought and been betrayed and died. Historically, as opposed to legend, there wasn't much known about him.

I said, 'Why extraordinary? He's a very evocative character.'

Again those rather frightening, protruding blue eyes fixed themselves on me. 'I'm Saxon, did you know that? Straight breeding. The name's changed, more's the pity, but not all that much. Hayward's simply a modern version of Hereward.' He paused. You could see a thought had struck him. 'So it's Hereward that's brought you to the fens? Þæt wæs gōd cyning! "A noble king, he was!"'

More brigand than king, but I wasn't going to argue, even though a Fenland farmer quoting *Beowulf* was a bit of a novelty.

I said, 'I like to get the feel of a place.'

He nodded. 'Agreed. So tell me, how does a writer become a policeman?'

I watched Smith and one of his companions working on the car. They were going about the job with a kind of unhurried competence, but even so it looked as though there was a lot of work to be done before the top of the gearbox came in sight. I thought gloomily that a little less brute force on my part and we'd have been fifty miles further on by now instead of sitting being interviewed by some dotty farmer who saw himself as living a thousand years ago.

It was Laurie who came to my rescue, and not for the

first time. 'I'm afraid it was the other way round.' She could be appallingly winsome if she tried. With acute embarrassment I heard her saying, 'Angus had been a policeman for *years* before his first book was published. It was just a hobby. It was terribly exciting when it turned out to be such a success.'

'Hah! Background's accurate too.'

Laurie smiled winningly. 'He's terribly painstaking over his research.'

'Like to talk about that.' Hayward swung back to me. 'What I don't understand is, why are you still a policeman?'

That was my business, damn it. All the same I made an effort. 'I like it, I suppose.'

'Doesn't it get boring, tramping round a beat all the time?'

Laurie said hurriedly, 'I don't think Chief Inspectors do much of that these days.'

'Oh! Chief Inspector is he? I didn't know.'

Smith came over, holding a piece of chromed metal in his hand, and very welcome he was. 'There's not much chance of a weld, I'm afraid. We'll have to make you a new stick.'

Well, that's the way it had looked from the start. I said, 'It's extraordinarily kind of you. Is it going to be much of a job?'

'I don't think so. We can turn most of it up on the lathe but the selectors need sorting out too. They'll take a little time. Not a difficult job—just fiddly.'

Hayward frowned. 'Best we can do, Straun. Where were you planning to stay the night?'

Like a fool I hesitated, because it hadn't been settled, and in the pause Sam, an extrovert child, joined in the conversation.

'We weren't planning anywhere,' he said cheerfully. Truthfully, too. 'You see, I've got an exeat from school, so Dad was just going to have a look round the fens till it got dark, then we'd head for the nearest town and stay there.'

Hayward didn't seem put out by the interruption. 'An excellent idea. Since you ended up here, you'd better stay with me.'

Pause. I avoided looking at Sam, in case my glance might do him some permanent injury. All my life I have had a marked distaste for staying at other people's houses, and over the years I have developed a number of near-foolproof reasons for refusing hospitality. Usually I plead a previously booked hotel, but not this time.

I said briskly, 'I wouldn't dream of it. You've been too kind already.'

'You haven't any option, come to that.' Hayward looked amused, which I suspected was out of character. 'Nowhere else to stay.' Then, rather uncannily reading my mind, 'You don't have to worry about getting under our feet, because I converted an old barn for guests a couple of years back. I'll tell my wife to open it up, then you'll be on your own.'

I added up the pros and cons in a kind of compressed flash. No way out. But anyway, it was uncommonly nice of him, so when I thanked him I truly meant it. Laurie, the civilized one, said, 'I do hope it's not going to mean a lot of extra work for your wife.'

'Lucy won't mind. Be glad of the company. Reminds me, I promised to buy her some stamps.' Hayward pulled himself to his feet. 'Give you a chance to see the village. Not a damn thing you can do here anyway. Smith'll give me a ring when your car's fixed.'

I went over and asked Smith if that was all right by him. I could see him deciding, but finally he nodded and smiled. 'It gives the boys a break from the B24. So don't worry, we can cope.'

I wasn't going to labour the point so I thanked him again and rejoined the others outside in the Land-Rover. Hayward's Saxon blood seemed to come to the fore once he was behind a steering-wheel because he drove the thing rather as if it was a war chariot. Stirring stuff. I tried to make small talk but the most I could gather was that the farmhouse was at the other end of the airfield and had been requisitioned as the officers' mess during the war. Parts of the perimeter track had almost given up the ghost but Hayward drove on at unslackened speed, the big tyres pounding from pothole to pothole. We reached the road and headed north. After a couple of miles a huddle of drab buildings broke up the everlasting flatness of the landscape.

'Wendal,' Hayward said. He drew up outside what was apparently both village shop and post office and we got out with him. The wide single street of the place was virtually deserted, although a few cars were parked here and there.

Laurie asked, 'Who actually *lives* here?'

It was a fair question, because the street must have been a couple of hundred yards long. There was a chapel and a garage with two pumps and a couple of tractors parked in the entrance. The remaining buildings were simple, slate-tiled cottages without any pretensions to design or beauty, although several of them had had the ground floor converted into some kind of business enterprise. *Doreen: Hair Styles, Sam's Videos*, a fish and chip shop called with rare wit *Charlie's Plaice*. There was also a notably unattractive public house called, for some obscure reason, the *Packet Boat*, which boasted a VW Golf parked at the door with an unexpected German number plate. Greasy papers discarded by clientele of *Charlie's Plaice* were picked up by the wind and blown along the road like tumbleweed. I looked both ways but there wasn't a living soul to be seen.

I saw Laurie turning to Hayward. 'The people who live here. What on earth do they *do*?'

'Independent farm hands, mainly.'

'Independent of what?'

Hayward said, 'They're self-employed. Most of them

own their own tractor, some have quite a bit of gear. When one of the local farmers wants a job done he hires someone by the hour. That way he doesn't have to pay a steady wage. Doesn't have to lay out money on machinery, either.'

'It doesn't sound like particularly steady work.'

Hayward shrugged those huge shoulders. 'It tops up their unemployment pay.'

Laurie frowned, an unsophisticated girl in some ways. 'But how do they draw unemployment when they're working?'

'Well, they don't tell the Ministry officials they're working, naturally.'

Laurie said primly, 'Well, I think that's dishonest.' She wandered away to look in at the window of Doreen of the hair styles.

'You offer free money to peasants,' Hayward said, 'and you can't expect them to turn it down.'

I was thinking over this profound thought when the door of the pub opened and a youth in jeans and a leather jacket came out at the run, heading our way. In a busy London street one would hardly have looked up. In what was apparently a deserted village the sudden noise and movement had the impact of an explosion. There was a confused babble of shouts from inside the building, then two large men emerged in pursuit. I watched indulgently. After all, anyone who lived in a place like Wendal could be forgiven a little horseplay now and then. Only maybe it wasn't just horseplay. I took a second look, because the pursuing men didn't look amused and there was something clutched in the youth's hand. Banknotes? Well, if the outside of the *Packet Boat* was anything to go by he wouldn't have got much.

'Gosh!' Sam observed from somewhere behind me. 'It was a hold-up!'

The youth spotted us and skidded to a stop, until a quick glance over his shoulder told him that the men behind him were hard on his heels. For a moment he didn't seem to know what to do. Then he took in Laurie, watching him with her back to the hairdresser's window, and he made a dash in her direction. Give him his due, he was quick. I don't think Laurie was even aware of what was happening before he'd reached her and dragged her in front of him. One arm was round her waist, the other feeling in his pocket. I thought briefly that he was simply stuffing the money away, but it wasn't just that. When the hand reappeared it was holding a flat-looking automatic.

'You get away from me! You hear?' When it came his voice was shrill. 'Get away or I'll blow her head off!'

CHAPTER 2

Policemen are trained in the craft of confrontation because most of their public image is based on just that. Drivers who object to having their car towed away, beaten-up wives, righteously offended pickpockets and whores accosted on their way to church are all eager for confrontation with the law. The law in its turn does its best not to let them down.

Maybe I was a poor pupil, maybe it had all got me on a wrong day. I knew perfectly well that you talk people into giving up a hostage, that if you go in with all guns firing your hostage is likely to end up dead. And Laurie was just such a hostage.

'Don't be a fool. Put that gun down.' Moving forward all the time, the last gunboat steaming in with a four-pounder blazing against a missile attack. It was a wonder the wretched boy didn't kill his victim then and there, simply my good luck that he was so surprised he actually shook his gun at me. He didn't shake it for long, because Laurie used that unguarded moment to jerk her head back hard into her captor's face. He yelped and let her go, which gave me the chance to grab his wrist and twist it back and up. I heard his shoulder joints crack and for a moment felt a fierce and shameful pleasure in the thought that I'd nearly broken his arm. The gun thudded to the ground.

My captive panted, 'All right! All right!'

He must have been eighteen or nineteen, black curly hair tied in a sort of mini-pigtail with a bit of ribbon. He was no beauty, the dirty olive of his skin gleaming with sweat, dark eyes wide with wariness and fear. Half a dozen men in working clothes had gathered round by now making appreciative noises, the talk-out having little popular appeal. I glanced round and could see people coming out of houses, drawn by whatever ant-like instinct it is that senses trouble from afar. I picked up the gun. For a moment I thought it was an Italian .25 Beretta but a second look confirmed that it was a non-firing replica. Well, the *Packet Boat* wasn't the first place to be held up by one of those and it wouldn't be the last. As a lookalike the thing was perfect.

I said to no one in particular, 'Better if we take him back inside.'

I sensed a fractional hesitation, then two large men took my charge off me and hauled him off back to the pub. To Laurie I said, 'Take Sam back to the car. I shan't be long.'

'I want to see what happens,' Sam said. No avail.

'Car,' Laurie said, and car it was.

The bar of the *Packet Boat* was not the Savoy but it offered a degree of comfort that was a good deal better than was suggested by the outside. Once off the beat of casual trade, the genuine English country pub is essentially practical, uncluttered by anything not directly concerned with the business of selling alcoholic drink. The *Packet Boat* bar was bright, carpeted and spotlessly clean. What appeared to be old-fashioned beer engines were obvious fakes but the brass gleamed and the beer glasses were more than oversize tumblers. On a fen winter's night it must have been unexpectedly welcoming and even in fen summer it was by no means bad. Well, to business. I pushed the pigtailed youth into a chair before he fell down.

'Anyone know who he is?'

'Aye. Darren Penney.' The landlord came out from behind the bar. A square man in his sixties with a short grey beard and a bad limp, sporting a loud checked shirt, sleeves buttoned at the wrists, no tie. *Bernard Sutton, licensed to sell wines, spirits and tobacco* had said the neat painted notice above the door.

A well-dressed young couple standing beside the bar eyed

him with interest. I heard the boy mutter in German that it looked as though they were going to have to wait for their drinks and the landlord got the drift with what must have been professional telepathy because he turned on them sourly.

'Bar's closed.'

The boy said amiably in English, 'There's no hurry.'

'If I say the bloody bar's closed, it's closed. Out.'

Exit German couple with dignity but tight-lipped. I had a feeling I wasn't the only one who was embarrassed but the law upholds the divine right of landlords to decide who gets served and who doesn't in their own pubs. But no wonder our tourist trade was going to the dogs. I made an effort and got back to Master Penney.

'Local?'

'Lives in a caravan with his dad. Only Harry's away most of the time since his wife ran out on him.'

'All right,' I said. 'What happened?'

'Didn't see it,' the landlord said unexpectedly. 'I were down the cellar. Ted, you saw it. Tell the gentleman what happened, Ted.'

Ted, a florid-looking chap in a moleskin jacket, bent to his task. 'Well, we were just havin' a drink when this young bugger comes in waving his gun around. Tells us all to keep back and goes over to the till and helps himself. Then Barney starts to come up from the cellar an' he runs out. Fred here tried to stop him an' got a clout for his pains.' Fred had indeed got the beginnings of a black eye.

I took the replica Beretta out of my pocket and turned to Darren Penney. 'Where did you get this?'

'Bought if off someone.' His hostility was tangible. 'Why shouldn't I? You don't have to have no licence for those.'

'Proper mad about guns and suchlike, he is,' Ted offered. 'Always buying and selling. You'd be surprised at the stuff you can still pick up around these old airfields, ammo and suchlike. The Yanks weren't careful with it, like our boys.'

'Old Davidson's seen what I got,' the boy told him. 'Said it was OK. I'm not bloody stupid.'

'Sergeant Davidson, from Easterham.'

Fair enough. Darren Penney's collection was local business, not mine.

'Well, you get the money back, at least.' I fished in Darren's pocket. Darren. I wondered which pop star had been named Darren at the time of Mrs Penney's unfortunate pregnancy. My hands closed round a fair-sized bundle of money and pulled it out for inspection—mainly five and ten pound notes. It seemed a hell of a lot of money to pick up from the till of a village pub.

I tossed the cash on the bar. 'Is that your usual day's takings, Mr Sutton?'

'Well then, it's a bit more than usual.' His voice had the slow, questioning lilt of Lincolnshire. 'But we had a couple of coach parties through this morning.'

It still seemed a lot of money, but then how much alcohol does the government let you buy for a fiver these days? I could feel the landlord's eyes on me, a wary character, but in his job he'd have to be. I said, 'Are you going to charge him?'

Nobody had been talking before, but the bar grew noticeably quieter. Somebody muttered something about the police.

Saul Hayward had been standing by the door minding his own business. Now people looked at him. He in turn nodded towards me. 'The gentleman here happens to be a police officer.'

A sure party-stopper that, even in the best of circles. In the *Packet Boat* they looked at me with even less enthusiasm than before. Then they looked away again.

I said, 'Mr Sutton, it was your money. Do you wish to press charges or not?'

'I've got the money back.' Barney Sutton picked up a glass and filled it with what looked like rather studied care. 'No charges.'

I got the feeling everyone let their breath out at the same time. I was about to say something but really what was the point? Policemen get used to battered wives telling them to mind their own business, just as they get used to biased or incompetent juries ignoring perfectly good evidence and acquitting villains whose guilt is almost ludicrously obvious. I glanced at the wretched Darren Penney. He didn't look surprised, but he didn't look particularly happy either, which I thought was a bit ungrateful of him.

'All right, Penney,' I said. 'You'd better clear out while the going's good.'

He stood up and stared about him, probably wondering if someone had made a mistake. Then he made a kind of bob to Hayward and scuttled out.

As Hayward and I followed him I said, 'One of these days that lad'll do something really nasty and you'll wish you'd stopped him while you had the chance.'

'Up to the landlord,' Hayward told me. 'Can't blame him for not wanting to get a local lad into trouble. Local lads are his bread and butter.'

I said, 'I should have thought that particular piece of gallows' bait was something he could do without. But it's his business, not mine.'

We went back to the Land-Rover and on to the farm house, one of those unexpectedly formal brick buildings with a low-pitched roof and square sash windows mathematically balanced on either side of a fan-headed door. What must at one time have been the stable block had been converted, rather well, into what was presumably a guest cottage and the whole thing was boxed within an uncompromising windbreak square of the inevitable planted cyprus.

'Get yourselves out,' Hayward said. 'I'll just find my wife.'

We got ourselves out and he found his wife walking in from the barns, a .22 rifle tucked under one arm which she'd presumably been using to keep down rats or whatever. A vast Irish wolfhound padded at her side. A nice lady, suitably and swiftly briefed.

'I think it's terribly kind of you to break down here. Since we got the cottage ready we've only had one lot of guests to stay, so it's marvellous being able to use it.' Lucy Hayward was a bit younger than her husband but not a lot, dressed in a check flannel shirt, a tweed skirt and green derriboots. Her hair, apparently un-tinted, was a wonderful russet, flecked with grey. As a girl, she must have been breathtaking. At fifty-something her face had softened but it hadn't sagged and if her skin didn't have the incandescent quality it may once have had it was still damn good. I wondered briefly why a such a beautiful woman should have married a weirdo like Saul Hayward, but what men and women find in their partners is usually a mystery to others, sometimes to themselves.

'I'll show you where everything is, then just give a shout if I've forgotten anything.' Lucy Hayward looked at Sam. 'I'm afraid we eat awfully early here. Dinner's in about half an hour. That be all right with you?'

Sam's eyes lit up, possibly with relief. Like most predators, he lived from meal to meal. 'Great!'

He eyed the shaggy monster of a dog admiringly. 'What's his name?'

'Beowulf.'

I should have guessed.

Farm building conversions tend to be either very good or very bad. The Haywards' was very good, intelligently planned and with enough but not too much of the original fabric left on show. Apart from a huge living-room, there

were three bedrooms, a couple of bathrooms and a galley
kitchen. The furniture was cheap and cheerful, the floors
covered in some kind of Berber cord, but there were bright,
decent prints on the walls, new paperbacks on the book-
shelves and a tray of drinks beside the wide brick fireplace.
Lucy Hayward exhibited the place at a brisk canter, then
made herself scarce.

'Nice,' Sam observed.

'It'll be nicer still when you've had a wash and changed
your clothes,' Laurie told him. She showed no signs of wish-
ing to be a surrogate mother but nevertheless she could
cope with Sam, probably better than I could.

'Which bedroom shall I have?'

'The end one.'

Really, life went on comfortably without help from me at
all.

'If it's absolutely vital to sleep out,' I said, 'this is hard
to improve on.' I had put my things in the far room, Laurie
in the centre. By common consent we never shared a room
when Sam was staying with us, probably a needless prudery
but there you are. I washed, put on a clean shirt before
going across to the farmhouse for dinner.

It was a strange meal. A good meal, as such meals go,
well served in pleasant surroundings, but a bit over-
shadowed by mine host. I kept remembering that Du Gues-
clin, that formidable Constable of France, had been
outstandingly ill favoured while Tiphane, his wife, had been
equally renowned for her beauty. Why did so many lovely
women get hitched to ugly men? Lucy's case seemed even
more extreme, because Hayward, quite apart from his
looks, was a bore. On his chosen subject, which seemed to
be the Fens, he was interesting, because nobody becomes a
fanatic without picking up a certain amount of information
on the way. But to have it all the time must have been
tiresome, particularly as, with most of his kind, he had the

knack of keeping the conversation flowing strictly one way. Mind you, I should never have asked him how long the farm had been in the family.

'The farm?' Hayward's blue chip eyes squinted at me as though assessing the parvenu sitting at his table. 'Gods! You think we only go back as far as that?'

Lucy Hayward said mildly, 'Mr Straun was only asking, dear.'

'All right. *All right!*' He shook the interruption off and turned back to me. 'Boadicea's Iceni were here first. Then the Romans. Then the Saxons. My forebears. No good talking about farms. This was a thousand years ago. Place was all fen. Water, bits of land here and there. Hah! Men got about on bloody great stilts. Lived among the reeds and killed any foreigner who poked his nose in.' Hayward sighed. 'Great days. All gone, though. Dutchman called Vermuyden came over and showed them how to drain the fens, about the time of Cromwell. Land dried out and people started farming it. Great-great-great-grandfather or something built this place about 1800.'

An awkward silence. Finally Laurie said, 'So no proper fens any more?'

'Still Wendal Fen.' Hayward's smile was suddenly sly and I felt sudden distaste. He said, 'Couple of miles beyond the old hangars. Bird reserve now or some such bloody nonsense, but it's real enough. Odd thing, it's deep. Why they left it, I suppose. Too much trouble to drain. In the old days they used to offer the Fen a life each year. Drowned a chap as a sacrifice. Supposed to make the crops grow.' He drew a deep breath. 'They say a plane went into the fen during the war. Never seen again. Odd place. But it's been ours for the best part of eleven hundred years. Morcar the Left-Handed took his death wound there when he seized it from Thorbold the Dane in 834. Morcar's burial ship's on this farm somewhere. If you dug deep enough you'd find his remains to this day.'

'And you are his direct descendant?'

'Oh yes.' Hayward looked surprised that I should ask. He pointed to an ancient blade, high on the wall. 'That was his sword. Morcar's sword.' He waggled huge fingers at me. 'As you have doubtless noted, I too am left-handed.'

I had noticed. Lots of people are left-handed. Still, it was interesting.

Lucy Hayward said suddenly, 'I believe you're fond of golf, Mr Straun.'

'Yes, I am.' True, too. And it got the chat bit away from her husband, which was doubtless intended. I asked, 'How did you know?'

'I read it on the dust jacket of your last book. It said you liked golf and Italian sports cars.'

I said, 'At the moment I'm not so sure about the sports cars.' She waited so I went on, 'Cars are a later thing. Something that came with making some unexpected money out of writing. But golf. There was a time I thought of nothing else. Used to follow the tournaments and hang around after a day's play in the hope of seeing what the big names looked like off the course.'

'You surprise me.'

'He's short-changing himself,' Laurie said. 'Angus wasn't just part of the crowd. He played in the Open himself once, as an amateur.'

A loyal soul. In Laurie's eyes I suppose I really had been good, whereas in mine I'd just been one more player who would never have made it as a professional. Like I was never going to make head of CID or win the Prix Goncourt. But then, as Laurie was apt to point out, I have something less than my ration of natural optimism.

Saul Hayward was saying, 'We've an interesting course

at Steeple Thurston. You might like to play a few holes while you're here.'

'That's a kind thought,' I told him. 'But there's young Sam to be considered. You see, we're taking him back to school.' I'd nothing against Steeple Thurston, wherever that might be, but I wasn't mad about a day's golf with Saul Hayward.

If I'd been counting on Laurie to back me up I counted in vain, because she said cheerfully, 'He's not due back at Blackthorne's for a couple of days. And we don't know when the car will be ready.'

Hayward nodded. 'Settled, then. I'll see when it can be arranged. I believe there's some American golf society visiting, which could make things a bit crowded. Can't stand societies myself, but I'm told they help keep subscriptions down.'

Golf societies tend to be the curse—or the blessing— of seaside clubs, interminable slow foursomes blocking the fairways for hours on end but swelling the coffers. But this wasn't the seaside, this was the Fens.

I asked, 'What brings them here? Wartime memories?' East Anglia had been stiff with American bombers in those days.

'Not veterans,' Hayward said. 'Just a society. They'll all be plumbers or vets or something. They come because the courses round here aren't crowded and the hotels give them a good deal. But they're not ex-servicemen, thank the gods.'

I wondered which gods he thanked. Thor? Odin? And what had he got against ex-servicemen?

Lucy said unexpectedly, 'I rather like them myself.'

Laurie frowned. 'Do you get many? I mean, they must be getting on, mustn't they?'

'My dear, they're in their seventies, mostly, and they come here in droves. You see them standing by the roadside with a map trying to find where their old PX stood, fifty years ago.'

'Loathe Americans,' Hayward said.

His wife said tranquilly, 'No, you don't. You quite liked the Shearers.'

'Visitors,' Hayward said shortly. 'I'm talking about the service people. They *invaded* us. For the first time since Duke William . . .' His voice trailed away, as though the memory was more than he could bear.

'Well, they come back as visitors now,' his wife told him briskly. She was pretty good with him.

'I suppose so.' Hayward didn't really want to be talked out of his obsession. With a good half of him living in Saxon times he must have seen the land as still vulnerable. I could imagine him still looking out for beacon fires in the night, warning that the Viking longboats were coming. Oh well.

'Some of the veterans bring their families with them,' Lucy was saying. 'Their tours are wonderfully organized.'

I tried to imagine the flat, inhospitable countryside alive with well-preserved World War Two pilots, all trying to evoke the past for their wives. I could make a pretty good picture of a lot of blue-rinsed grandmothers doing their best to look enthusiastic about a semi-circle of cracking concrete.

'*Look, honey, a dispersal!*'

Well, they'd fought that war, which was more than I'd done. All we were doing was knocking the memories we didn't have.

Laurie said, 'Time Sam got to bed.' She had an enviably relaxed relationship with my son, whom she treated as an equal up to and including bedtimes, when it was accepted that between equals there should be no messing about. I sensed, uncomfortably, that her touch was a good deal surer than mine.

'You'll have a brandy with me before you go,' Hayward said. But Laurie and Sam were off, so we had thirty-year-old Armagnac on our own while Saul Hayward talked of the Fens and warriors a thousand years in their graves.

When I got back to the cottage Sam was long asleep and Laurie was lying on top of her bed in a dressing-gown, reading a manuscript. She was always reading manuscripts, and sometimes I wondered if literary agents ever got to read a printed book. But she dropped the thing on her lap as I came and held out a hand.

'How was he?'

I sat down on the bed beside her. 'If you don't happen to be interested in the politics of the Fens under William I, he's a crashing bore. As I am, he's good value.'

'Strong on Hereward the Wake?'

'A bit too strong, if anything. Opinion isn't fact.'

'Do you really want to go over and play golf with him?'

I said, 'I wouldn't mind. But I don't want to leave you stuck here.'

'Sam and I will be all right. And I rather like Lucy.'

I rolled off the bed and went over to the window. There was a big moon but across the endless fields a mist was rolling in. No more than a couple of feet from the ground, it was encroaching stealthily, like a tide. I watched it soften the outline of a distant fence, pour silently down a bank, fill up a ditch and creep up the other side. Presently it reached the northernmost line of trees that marked the boundaries of Hayward's farmhouse. For a while they seemed to act as a barrier and I half expected the mist to turn aside and roll on down the road, but a few probing wisps crept between the trees and edged their way on to the lawn. Within minutes the breach was complete and the flowerbeds engulfed. I shivered, which was unlike me.

Behind me, Laurie asked, 'What's the matter? Are you cold?'

'No,' I said. 'Just getting spooked. It's funny country at night.'

'I loathe it. It gives me the creeps.'

I turned to look at her. 'Truly?' She was not given to creeps or fancies.

'Truly. I feel it even in daylight. The feeling that the place resents your being here.'

I thought of the odd crowd in the *Packet Boat* bar. 'I must admit the people aren't overwhelmingly friendly.'

'I'm not talking about the people, it's the place itself.' She took off her glasses and fiddled with them, something she did rarely, not being a fiddler. Without the big lenses she looked younger and uncharacteristically vulnerable. She went on in a low voice, 'I remember there was a huge wood near my school. There were glades and paths round the edges where people used to have picnics but there wasn't really any way of getting into the middle. People said nobody had ever walked across the woods from one side to the other, but of course that was nonsense. Two of us tried it one weekend.'

'What happened?' Difficult to imagine Laurie as a school-girl, though not that many years ago.

'We got a fair way in. We'd got some confetti from some-where and laid a trail behind us so that we could find our way out, so it wasn't very scary. I think we were a bit disappointed. Then we came to a rather pretty little clear-ing.' She paused and looked at me. 'Angus, it was terrifying! A most enormous sense of—evil. Jane and I both felt it. I remember her saying, "Let's get out of here" and we tried to beat an orderly retreat, but it didn't last. Half a dozen steps and we ran. Didn't stop running till we got back to the edge of the wood.'

So they were a couple of hysterical schoolgirls, expecting horrors and finding them. Though granted it was hard to imagine Laurie ever being hysterical. I said, 'You mean you feel that way here?'

'Not as strong. Of course not. But it reminds me.'

I turned back to the window. She was right, the place
had an atmosphere but perhaps that was its attraction. I
could imagine the Norman William doing his best to cope
with this part of England, in the days when it was an area
of marsh and water, interspersed with islands of land and
inhabited by murderous fanatics. I liked the idea of Hereward as a kind of resistance leader, loved by the people,
betrayed by the priests. A kind of Robin Hood. Maybe
that's all Hereward was, apart from legend.

Outside, beyond the mists of the garden, something
screamed.

Laurie jumped. 'For God's sake! What was that?'

If I'd known I wouldn't have felt the hairs rising on the
back of my neck. 'A weasel getting a rabbit?' No great
countryman, even I knew that as nonsense, because no
rabbit shrieked like that unless it was Harvey.

Echoing my thoughts again, Laurie said, 'It would have
to be a big rabbit.'

I stared out over the mist-fuzzy outline of the garden,
but nothing moved. I told myself that we were in deepest
rural England, where nature wasn't made up of fat tabby
cats with collars and names like Samantha. Out here, predators still stalked and slew their prey, and the sounds of
nature were not toned down for family listening. Just the
same, I knew I was going out to have a look.

I said, 'I won't be a minute.'

'You said yourself it was a rabbit . . .' Laurie reached
out and grabbed me, unusual but not unpleasant.

I said, 'And you didn't believe that any more than I did.'
I paused. I didn't really want to go outside, because I didn't
want to make a fool of myself, chasing some everyday spot
of natural selection. But policemen are brought up to stick
their noses into other people's business and early training
dies hard. I said, 'I shan't be a minute.'

It was colder outside than I'd expected, a damp chill

from the mist after the heat of the day. I walked across the garden and looked back at the cottage floating on a kind of vapour mattress, the effect being not unlike a Hammer film, with Count Dracula waiting in the wings. It was uncannily quiet, and I guessed that the local wild life had decided that what with one thing and another this was no night for hunting.

I pushed on through the trees, wondering just what I was expecting to find. Why was I here anyway? A line of sawn-off willows loomed ahead of me, edging a waterway like a Rackham illustration of something in the Wild Wood. I was beginning to understand the feelings of Mole, pottering about in places best left alone. It occurred to me that I had done whatever was expected of me and could honourably go back home after making a circuit of the first clump of willow.

I made the circuit. Darren Penney crouched before me.

Difficult to say which of the two was the more startled. The last time I'd seen the wretched boy he'd been sitting doing his bored bit in the *Packet Boat* bar. He didn't look very cocky now. His face was chalk white in the moonlight and his eyes seemed enormous as his left hand gripped his right wrist, from which the hand hung down in a limp mess. Blood trickled from the fingers, the knuckles a blue black pulp as though they'd been smashed with a hammer.

I said, 'For God's sake, boy—'

I don't know whether he registered shock or horror or pity in my voice but whatever it was it didn't seem to inspire much confidence. He said something to me but the words didn't make sense, it was no more than the guttural protest of an animal in pain. Then he turned, stumbling, to vanish in the mist.

CHAPTER 3

Breakfast is a time when few are at their best. I for one was not at my most diplomatic, nor wanting to be for that matter. The subject of the wretched Darren Penney irked me and I saw no reason why it should be ignored, so I recounted my experience of the night before.

'Sounds as though someone gave him what he deserved,' Saul Hayward announced once I'd described the boy's injuries. 'Appropriate, I'd say.'

'So's cutting a thief's hand off,' I told him. 'It's still not something you do in a civilized society.' It takes practice to sound pompous while stating the obvious and I was conscious that I'd done it in one.

My host stared at me balefully over a forkful of fried egg and I felt a certain tension on the part of our respective womenfolk. Laurie, I suspected, would have kicked me had I been within range but I wasn't. Hayward said, 'Could have been an accident. Stuck his hand in a harvester or something.'

'In the middle of the night?'

'So you think someone smashed his hand deliberately?'

I said, 'Either someone did just that or his getting injured is one hell of a coincidence.'

Hayward didn't argue that one. 'Well, in these parts people like to settle things for themselves. Young Penney's a useless young lout and you know as well as I do that if it had been dealt with officially some fool of a magistrate would simply have said it was all due to his deprived childhood or something. Then they'd have given the police a roasting for bringing the case to court at all.'

His wife looked at him with that kind of calm beautiful

women seem to have made their own. 'Really, Saul, I do think you exaggerate. Mr Straun will think we're living in the Middle Ages.'

'Don't be a fool, Lucy.'

Usually it's embarrassing to listen to men being rude to their wives, here not so, Saul Hayward being the kind of man who spoke the same to everyone and Lucy a woman who only took offence when seriously intended. But I remembered the reluctance of the pub regulars to do anything about young Penney, an unlikely reaction if ever there was one. Maybe Hayward was right, and they'd simply waited until I was out of the way before sorting him out. I didn't know, nor was I likely to. Their affair, not mine, thank the Lord. Another day and Laurie and I would be out of Wendal Fen for good.

Sam said with the apostrophe of someone immersed in their own line of thought, 'Mr Smith said that Laurie and I could go down and have a proper look at his B-24 this morning.'

'Did he?' It was news to me but keeping abreast of eight-year-olds tends to be a full-time job anyway.

Laurie said mildly, 'He did, as a matter of fact. I think he saw Sam was impressed.'

'Well, I suppose that's all right.' I made a token hesitation in deference to the Haywards. I was hardly expecting to be entertained but it felt awkward sitting there at their breakfast table and organizing our day round them, so to speak.

'I should go,' Lucy said. 'Patrick's completely obsessed with aircraft, of course, but he's terribly nice. Interesting, too. I'd come with you if I hadn't got to go to Wisbech.'

'OK,' Laurie said. She looked at me. 'What about you?'

'Working for me this morning,' Saul said unexpectedly. 'If he doesn't mind.'

'No.' Surprised, I said, 'No, I don't mind. But I warn

you, my knowledge of farming is limited.' If I had to pay for a night's lodging in some way it was fair enough. But I had a prickle of disquiet. Be you candlemaker or undertaker, there's always someone waiting to get your services in exchange for a drink and a merry quip. Was I, after all, going to be called upon to do something about the wretched Darren?

'No, I don't want you to solve a crime.' Hayward actually managed a sort of laugh, showing strong yellowing teeth, like a horse. Either he could mindread or he'd had the same kind of conversation with policemen before. He coated toast with a quarter of an inch of cholesterol. 'There's a visitor calling this morning. American. Be glad if you'd look after him.'

I waited to see if there was any more but Hayward had started to eat his butter-covered toast. His wife caught my eye and smiled gently. 'Saul woke up this morning with sciatica. It took him half an hour to get into that chair and it'll probably take even longer to get him out. He couldn't show anyone round the place if his life depended on it.'

I felt sympathy. No sufferer myself, but I remembered coming upon Murdoch, my father's gardener, leaning rigid over his fork, powerless to move, his face shiny with sweat. At the time he'd described his troubles as 'a wee go of the screws', and though I'd never heard the term before it had stuck, that and Murdoch's face, he being no softie and something of a hero to Master Angus aged about ten.

'I'll do my best,' I said, the usual facile promise of the incompetent. 'What do you want me to do with him?'

Hayward gave the short bark that apparently counted as laughter. 'Don't imagine you'll have to do anything apart from keeping him company. Apparently he was stationed on the airfield here during the war, so he's come back to have a look at it. Typical American sentimentality.'

I said, 'I'm surprised you invited the man. You said yourself that you can't stand Americans.'

Pause while we eyed each other.

'I can't.'

'So?'

'The club president asked me. Difficult to refuse.'

Well, I suppose it was, golf clubs being the same the world over. In a perverse way, I warmed to him. 'All right,' I said, 'what do I have to do?'

Hayward peered at me as though trying to discover whether the offer was genuine. Without letting me in on his conclusions he added, 'I expect he'd enjoy it if you played a few holes with him. I gather he was instrumental in having it laid out in the first place. He was a golfer of some renown.'

'And his name?'

'His name,' Saul Hayward said, 'is Frank Albatross Segal.'

Albatross: a large sea-bird. Also, in golf-speak, a double eagle or three under par. I tried to tie those two facts into the reality of ex-Captain Segal standing there beside the car someone had lent him, his pale blue linen slacks matching his windcheater. He was shortish but broad-shouldered and the stomach behind the expensive buffalo hide belt was flat as a board. If he'd been a flier during the war he couldn't have been much under seventy but he'd been so well maintained over the years that if he'd been a car he might still have been in warranty. His broad, Slavic face had the overall coffee tint of years in a good climate and his smile said a lot for his dentist. If Albatross Segal had really been a used car I'd have bought him like a shot and to hell with the mileage.

'Mr Segal?'

'Just call me Al, everyone does.' His grip was dry and firm. 'You'll be Mr Hayward?'

No, I was not Mr Hayward. I made the explanations and led him to the Land-Rover. As we climbed aboard I asked him how many there were in his party.

'Ten.' He took out a pair of Ray-Bans and gave them a polish. 'Most of them are real estate agents. Nice people.'

'Did any of them fly round here?'

Albatross Segal shook his head. 'Nope. Most of them too damn young anyway. But someone found out I'd been posted with the 901 Bombing Squadron right here and they said I'd gotta come and look the old place up.'

'They say you like your golf.'

'Sure do.' He glanced around. 'Used to be a little nine-hole here where we used to play a bit between missions. We made it up round the outside of the perimeter track.'

'It's still here,' I told him. 'Part of it, anyway. Mr Hayward tells me he uses it for practice now and then.'

Segal looked happy. 'I heard something like that but thought it was too good to be true. It's been a long time, a real long time. I'd sure as hell like to play it again. Brought my clubs, just in case.'

'You'd better get them.'

He went back to his car and returned with a worn bag and a lot of Ben Hogans, good clubs but older than I'd expected. Segal must have seen me look at them because he said apologetically, 'Don't get to play much these days.'

'Who does?' I dumped the gear in the back. 'What shall we do? Have a look round and play later?'

He nodded. 'That'll be best.'

I said, 'Then you'd better tell me where to go. That is, if you can remember your way around.'

'I was here two years,' Segal said. 'I guess I ain't forgotten.'

I got out from behind the wheel. 'In that case you know

more about the place than I do. You'd better drive.'

You can't get inside someone else's memories, but even from the outside they're not unmoving. We drove out on to the road, back towards the village for perhaps half a mile before Segal swung in at what I guessed was the main entrance to the farm. There were concrete gateposts but the gates themselves were long gone. A vast tractor stood on the hard standing, its diesel thudding to itself while its driver did something to the yellow-painted complex of tanks and piping tied on behind. He looked up, recognized the Land-Rover but not the driver, nodded. Going out, he might have wondered. Coming in was probably all right.

Segal slowed. 'That used to be the guard house.'

Guard house would presumably translate as guard room. I looked at the building behind the tractor. Stained grey wash and a rusting roof of corrugated iron, the look of a long-neglected beach chalet, even down to the remains of a wildly incongruous verandah. I'd seen a dozen identical buildings at the entrance to a dozen similar farms and never thought much about them. But of course. There were faded letters on the wall, ancient graffiti, the half-century-old flotsam of an ancient war. An 'A' and 'REP' and further down a couple of 'Os'. Segal saw where I was looking.

'All personnel report to Guard House,' he explained. He gave the building a look of grudging admiration. 'Still there. They built the place good.'

We drove on round the concrete track circling God knows how many acres of sugar beet, pausing briefly at half a dozen rectangles that had been part of the quartermaster's empire, a level stretch of ground that had been the site of the enlisted men's domestic quarters, four bare corner columns still supporting the roof of what had been the PX.

'Baled hay,' Segal said. 'They got the PX full of baled hay.'

'It hasn't been a PX for nearly fifty years,' I reminded

him. 'You could hardly expect Saul Hayward to fill it with Coke.'

'I guess not.' I could see he was disappointed, but even if Hayward hadn't flattened them, most of the hastily thrown up wartime buildings would have gone by now. As it happened, Wendal Fen was a better bet than most.

I said, 'Some of the hangars are still here. There's someone rebuilding a B-24 in one of them.'

'Yeah. So they said.' Segal swung off the perimeter track and hit a runway. It was a hundred feet wide and from the centre, which was where Segal was driving, it looked like nothing so much as a huge road. I began to realize for the first time just how much land must have been sacrificed during the war so that bombers could make those lethal runs over the North Sea. A field the size of the strip in front of me would have been a significant thing, whereas a prairie of concrete was nothing much at all unless you planned to start a turkey farm on top of it. No wonder nine farmers out of ten went to the expense of breaking the things up.

'You know,' Segal said, 'it looks kind of funny from down here.'

'You must have driven over it often enough before.'

'Sure,' Segal said, 'but that's not what you remember.'

I supposed not. Not for the first time, the odd feeling of inadequacy, the benchmark between men who have fought in war and those who haven't. The Maserati and a good deal more besides was paid for by my spare time novel-writing, plots all ankle deep in the blood of ancient wars. I was even a sort of authority on mediæval weaponry, but it didn't alter the fact that as I drove up the one-time runway of Wendal Fen that day I'd have liked to have remembered the kind of things that Albatross Segal was remembering.

He said, 'They left the control tower.'

'I think they still fly the odd plane—Smith and his friends,' I told him. 'I suppose they'd need it.'

Segal shook his head. 'No, not with one plane, they wouldn't need it.' He looked at me. 'They fly the B-24?'

'They plan to. I imagine only test flights so far.'

'Maybe we could look in on them after we've hit a ball or two?'

'They'd like to see you,' I said, and meant it.

The control tower didn't seem to be used for anything much. At some time in the past there'd been a fire and the decaying concrete was chipped and blackened. There were still stairs to the top but no floor to speak of, but we went on up. In films the walls of old wartime buildings always bear the faded legend of the departed, the squadron state on the day operations ended, a pin-up of Betty Grable. If the walls of the concrete box had ever been so decorated the wind and rain through the unglazed windows had long scoured it bare.

'Come have a look,' Segal said.

There was a kind of balcony outside what had once been the square glass box on the top of the tower. House martins had made nests along the edge of the roof and droppings of years left the walkway slippery and foul, but Segal wasn't paying much attention to his footwear, he was looking out over the runway, so I looked too. Lincolnshire is a flat county, so just being on top of the old control tower made us pretty high. You could see the dark green of Hayward's beet, and the crop pattern of just about everybody else for as far as the eye could see. There were no hedges to the fields, and precious few trees. There was a water tower here and there, the marching pylons of the electricity grid, the hard straight black line of a dyke. Curiously, only the broad stripe of the old runway, with the hangars grouped as a distant background seemed real, and for the first time I found myself wanting to ask Segal what it had been like. At that moment I really wanted to know, but then I realized that there are some things that just aren't picked up second hand.

I said, 'Do you want to have a look at the golf course?'

'Sure. Why not?' He turned away from whatever it was he'd been looking at and slapped the cement facing of the wall in front of him. A piece of it broke off under his hand and he held it up for inspection. 'You see that?'

'Yes.'

'Let's go see if the grass has lasted better.'

He was silent as we went back down the stairs. I could see a Dinky-car-sized tractor working its way across a field that must have been a good mile away, but the thud of its diesel sounded as though it were next door. I wondered what sounds Segal heard. It occurred to me that my going round with him was an intrusion and I resented Hayward foisting me on to someone who would have been happier with his memories without someone like me looking on. Too late now. We drove back along the perimeter track, dodging bits of farm machinery, to the hut I'd noticed the day before, a little hut beside the first tee.

Segal walked over to it while I got the clubs out of the back. He stood looking towards the green, which must have been about two hundred and fifty yards away. He didn't say anything. Finally I asked him if it was much as he remembered it.

'I remember it fine. Hasn't hardly changed at all.' He took his bag from me. 'Seems I got it about right when I laid her out. Mow the greens and that's about it.'

Well, yes. I could see that originally the course was simply nine holes, laid out one after the other outside the airfield's perimeter track where there was a border of waste-land extending up to the Faversham road. It was perhaps seventy yards wide, covered in coarse grass that was kept short by a few sheep who studied us incuriously. The first hole, which I guessed would be much like all the rest, was

hardly exciting. There were a couple of bunkers guarding
the green, but apart from that the only real hazard was if
you hooked a ball across the road and into the scrubby
expanse of willows beyond. It was basic stuff, but it was a
lot better than nothing and I could understand Saul Hayward keeping up a few holes for his own entertainment. All
it needed was someone with a mower once a week and a
biggish farmer wasn't likely to be short of an odd bod to do
that.

Out of the blue I said, 'Why do they call you Albatross?'

Segal stopped fiddling with his clubs and looked at me.
'You mean you don't know?'

Well, no. Why should I? 'No,' I said, 'nobody told me.'

'Sure. Why should they?' Segal considered. 'It was back
in 1944 and I guess there was a kind of drive on at the time
to keep relationships good between US servicemen and the
British. You know what I mean?'

I nodded. There'd been a fair amount of tension between
the English and their major Allies, most of it stemming
from the uninhibited admiration of English womanhood for
American servicemen.

'So they fixed up this match: Yanks versus the Brits. Any
of the guys in 8th and 9th TAF against the RAF crews in
the same area. Seventy-two holes up the road at Steeple
Thurston.' Segal selected a ball from his bag and teed it
up, then took a three wood, gave it what seemed to me a
faintly regretful look before replacing it with a driver. It
struck me suddenly that back in the 1940s he must have
played this particular hole a hundred times and always
with a small wood.

'One isn't the man one once was, Mr Straun.'

'Angus,' I said. 'And none of us is, come to that.'

Those strange blue eyes studying me out of that East
European face. 'Ever strike you that maybe it's just as well?'
He looked back at the job in hand and drove. Not one to

waggle over the ball or threaten it with practice swings, he just gave the thing an unfriendly look and hit it. And by no means badly. A little stiff on the follow through but straight up the middle, a comfortable wedge short of the green.

I took a three wood, too, not because I was particularly long with it, more by reason of the fact that I can be a bit wild with a driver and I didn't fancy ending up in the road. With the ground as hard as it was I didn't need to worry about length, and I landed only a couple of yards behind my opponent.

'You were saying about Yanks versus Brits.'

'Yeah. Well, on the last day I was trailing two strokes behind the leader, an RAF sergeant.' The Albatross picked up his bag and walked light-footedly after his ball. 'That was after the seventeenth.' He paused. It must have been a story he'd been through often enough to know where the good bits were. 'Maybe I should tell you the sergeant's name was Bob Bannerman. You heard of him?'

I jumped. 'Heard of him? Christ, I played with him once myself. He won the Open two years running, in 1940 and '41.'

'You did?' Segal appraised me and I knew that somewhere in that drip-dry brain he was noting that if such a game had taken place at all I must have been very young and Bob Bannerman way past his best.

'It was in a Pro Am,' I told him. 'I was nineteen and Bob Bannerman must have been in his fifties by then. He beat the hide off me.'

'Nice guy.'

'Yes.' In a way he'd been a hero of mine, the young having a weakness that way. Every boy's idea of a jolly good chap, the sportsman supreme, *sans peur et sans reproche*. I'd forgotten that he'd finished the war as a physical training expert in the RAF. We reached our balls and paused. I said, 'So what happened?'

'On the eighteenth?' Segal fished out his wedge. 'Bannerman got his par.'

'And you?'

'The eighteenth at Steeple Thurston's a par 5. I got an albatross, which meant I won by a stroke.'

Any albatross has to be some kind of fluke, because even a short par 5 is more than four hundred and fifty yards from tee to pin. A good drive of two hundred and fifty yards and you're left with only one stroke with which to hit the ball almost as far again and end up with it in the hole. It should be impossible, of course, yet every now and again it gets done. Mr Segal had done it, and thereby beaten the Open champion. No wonder they called him Albatross.

'Al,' Segal said, reading my thoughts as usual. 'Most times people just call me Al.' He took a nine iron and skied his ball high on to the green about ten feet from the pin. I used a sand wedge for mine but the result was about the same, apart from the fact that he missed his putt and I holed mine.

I said, 'How did it feel to have beaten the Open champion?'

'Pretty good.' Segal looked reflective. 'Still remember it. Bob Bannerman does too, come to that.'

I said, 'I didn't even know he was still alive.'

'Hell, yes. Lives in these parts, they tell me.' Segal looked surprised that I didn't know. 'The boys at Steeple Thurston laid on a kind of party for us. Bob was there. Your honour.'

No. 2 round the perimeter of Wendal Fen was very much like No. 1 only shorter. I gave my ball a clip with an eight and got it to the heart of the green. 'Tell me,' I said, 'just how good were you?'

Segal bared those even white teeth of his. 'Pretty good, I guess. My old man was a pro at the local country club and I kind of picked it up from him. Leastwise I was playing scratch when I was fifteen.' He flipped his ball beside mine.

I suspected that at seventy he was probably still playing to single figures. 'But sure, I was on a lucky streak.'

'Given the albatross was luck,' I said, 'you were still only two strokes behind the champion.'

Segal shrugged his shoulders. 'He was two strokes ahead and I reckon he thought that was enough. That kind of game, he didn't want to run away with it.'

The same thought had occurred to me but I hadn't wanted to mention it. 'So what happened after that?'

'After that, I was tour-expired. I'd done my twenty-five missions, so I went back to the States. Took an English girl with me for a bride and cashed in on the fact that as a golfer I was news.'

'You turned pro?'

'Hell, no!' Segal looked pained. 'Used it to get into college. In those days there were plenty of pretty good places that would take an ex-serviceman if his sport record was good enough and to hell with whether he could read and write. I made Harrington an offer and they swallowed me up. I took business studies. Came out and went into the real estate business.' He paused. 'Did all right, too.'

'In other words,' I said, 'that one albatross changed your life.'

We putted out for a half. 'You could say that,' Segal said. 'Yes, sir, you could say that.' He picked the balls out of the hole, tossed me mine. His eyes went past me, across the road. There was a house there, among the willows. Not an empty shell like the control tower, but in need of a good deal of care and attention. Segal said, 'That was a pub in my day. "The *Swallow*."' He pushed his putter back into its bag. 'Let's go in.'

Here's a church. Let's go in. Now who said that? My subconscious dredged up Mr Wemmer in *Great Expectations*. Aloud I said, 'It's probably boarded up.'

'Maybe.' Segal laid his golf bag down beside the tee and

struck off across the rough. It wasn't far. Fifty yards took us to the road and another hundred to the house. It wasn't particularly old but there's an air about buildings that have been used for licensed premises. I looked up at the wall above the front door and there, sure enough, were a couple of sizeable holes where a sign had once been. Albatross Segal was snuffling round the back like a beagle and by the time I reached him I heard the creak of a door opening. Perhaps it had been open all the time or maybe Segal had given it a crafty push.

I followed him in. The downstairs was dark but the light filtered through the cracks in the plywood shuttering was sufficient to find one's way around. And of course Segal had been right, the place had indeed been a pub, as a bar and a lot of advertisements stuck to the wall proved. Cleaned out, deprived of furniture, a pub looks remarkably like a stage set, but Segal could have given it only a cursory glance before I heard his feet creaking on the stairs.

I said, 'You'd better watch where you're walking. Those boards sound as though they could break under you.'

He didn't answer and I heard him pause on the landing. I went after him, but by the time I'd got to the head of the stairs he'd vanished. I looked round. The place had been a pretty typical small inn with accommodation for the land-lord and his family plus three or four spare rooms for the odd overnight guest. Quite close by I heard the squeal of rusty hinges and sunlight splashed across the dusty boards. Segal was in one of the rooms on my right and I went after him. Who the present owners were I'd no idea but I couldn't imagine they'd be pleased at having their property opened up without their knowledge.

'You know something?' he was saying. 'The view. It ain't changed in all these years.'

The floor creaked as I went in, boards covered in yel-lowed newspapers put down to stop dust coming up through the carpet. There were pink cabbage roses on the walls, with lighter, squared-off shapes where pictures had hung, a rather nice old Victorian cast-iron fireplace and a cheap electric fire with a rusted reflector that hadn't been worth enough to take away. Segal had pushed open the window and was standing looking out over what must have been the willow thickets and the road and Hayward's farm beyond, though from where I stood all I could see was the American's dark silhouette against the square of yellow sunlight that was the window-frame.

'You know something?' Segal said.

'No?'

But he never got round to telling me. I heard the smack of the head shot what seemed minutes before the sound of the rifle itself. The impact threw Segal back against the corner of the wall and for an instant I took in the blue-black smudge in the centre of his forehead, the bloody haze as the bullet tore its way out of the back of his skull, and last of all the blank, frozen look of the Albatross's face as he died standing up, folded his wings and dropped out of his sky.

CHAPTER 4

There is a curious No-Man's-Land feel about one's room in somebody else's house. A safe haven, where one can say what one likes about one's host. A not safe haven because family business needs to be conducted with sufficient discretion to ensure smiling faces at breakfast. Thus caution that night when Laurie announced that she would take Sam back to school the following day.

I said, 'We'll have to rent a car. God knows where from.'

'It's all right. Patrick will take us.'

'Patrick?'

'Patrick Smith.' She was in bed, looking particularly fetching, I thought, in a large-sized man's pyjama top, broad stripes, red on black. I wondered if she wore them on her own, or simply for my benefit, ungenerous thought. It is a cliché that girls look sexy in men's clothes, but clichés get to be clichés because they are true.

'The chap who's fixing the plane.' I was sitting on the end of the bed, my mind on several things at once.

Laurie frowned slightly, not impressed by these parrotlike repetitions, not realizing that it had been a conscious effort on my part to remember who the man was. She said, 'Yes, the chap who's fixing the plane. Sam wanted to watch him so we paid him a visit. He said we should—remember?'

'Yes,' I said. I didn't, though. 'How's the Khamsin getting on?'

'I don't know. It's not ready. But Sam was telling Patrick how his exeat was up tomorrow and he said he'd to go into Peterborough tomorrow anyway. He'd take us along. I mean, the school's only a few miles from there.'

A twinge of the old green-eyed monster. 'How did the good Patrick know I couldn't go?'

Laurie's grey eyes homed in on me from behind the big glasses. 'He didn't. He expected you to come too. But since you can't, it makes even more sense if Sam and I go.'

'Well, yes,' I agreed. 'It's very good of him.' Sam's school was at Warnock, about six miles this side of Peterborough. At least it wouldn't take Smith out of his way. I said, 'There's a police car from Lincoln picking me up at nine.'

Laurie pulled a face. 'I don't see why they couldn't have come and talked to you here.'

Well, neither did I, come to that, but they'd more or less taken it for granted I'd go there and at least they were providing the transport. I said, 'Not my patch. I suppose it's just their way of doing things.'

'It was obviously an accident.'

I thought of Albatross Segal with his brains splashed on the window-frame. The police had arrived from Lincoln pretty smartish, asked questions, taken pictures and generally behaved in a responsible manner. As Laurie said, it was obviously an accident, what else? Country folk are notoriously slap-happy with their firearms, blasting off with little thought for where the odd wild shot may land. *I fired some buckshot into the air, it came to earth I know not where.* Only it hadn't been buckshot, it had been .22. But every farmer's son used those for potting vermin.

'Yes,' I said, 'it's just a formality, but I'd better go. I *was* there when it happened, after all.'

'You'll say goodbye to Sam in the morning?'

I said sharpish, 'Of course I'll say goodbye to him before he goes back.' It came out a bit crisper than I'd intended but I was feeling guilty about the whole thing and Laurie knew it. The difficulties weren't insurmountable. Probably if I was firm about it the Lincoln police would put my report off for a day, and if I dug around, Wendal Fen would doubtless yield a car that I could either rent or borrow. The truth was that I'd just seen a man shot dead in front of me. He hadn't been my responsibility and the chances were the thing was an accident anyway, but I was a policeman and I couldn't help it if at this moment Sam had slipped back into place number two.

'Right,' Laurie said. 'Just as long as we know.'

Come the morning, of course, Sam couldn't have cared less whether I accompanied him back to school or not. There were times when I was pretty sure he found Laurie superior entertainment anyway. This morning it was academic as we were both sharing second fiddle to Patrick Smith, who was nothing to do with the police or books but devoted himself very properly to rebuilding aeroplanes. I allowed myself to be taken off to Lincoln with a conscience, if not clear, somewhat less niggly than it had been.

Lincoln is an ancient city mounted precariously on the only hill for miles around. It has a cathedral, the remains of a castle and a Superintendent called Thomas Higham, red-haired, fattish and a local man who struck me as full of good sense.

'Considerate, getting himself knocked off in front of a copper. One gets a better report that way.' His shrewd, piggy eyes looked me over. 'You're quite happy about it?' He meant happy about it being an accident, not happy about Segal getting his brains blown out.

I said, 'We haven't had the feedback from the Americans yet. Grosvenor Square is liable to think their visiting nationals are entitled to a bullet-free vacation.'

'If you were run over by a bus in a foreign country, would you imagine the British Government making a fuss?'

I said, 'No. Come to that, if a British plane was shot down over a foreign country and its passengers cooked and eaten, I wouldn't expect our people to send more than a stiff note.'

Higham's little mouth puckered into a smile. 'I shan't quote you, Chief Inspector. But you're answering what wasn't the question.'

I said, 'The answer to your question is, "No, I'm not at all happy about it."'

'You think it was not an accident?'

'Let's put it this way,' I said. 'I think it's a very odd accident.' I surprised myself with the readiness with which I could recall the smack of the bullet on skin-covered bone. I went on, 'A .22 cartridge throws a bullet about the same size as an air-rifle slug. It's got a bit more steam behind it but it's what farmers give their twelve-year-olds for killing bunnies. This particular .22 didn't just penetrate Segal's skull, it blew the back of his head off.'

Higham joined his fingers together and made a little house. 'Maybe it was a long .22. High velocity.'

'I should think it most certainly was,' I agreed. 'But why? If you're potting vermin you don't need more than a short load. Besides, farmers aren't all that irresponsible. If there's a chance of them missing a squirrel they take damn good care they're not going to throw a bullet into the next county.'

'The young don't give a damn, boy.' Superintendent Higham put up his index fingers and turned his little house into a church. 'Had this case last month—a young lad pinched a car and killed a girl who was standing waiting for a bus. "Poor boy," some social worker said to me. "Poor boy, he'll have it on his conscience for the rest of his life." Conscience! The little bastards haven't got any conscience. That one had nicked three more cars before his hearing even came up.'

Well, I could see his point. I said, 'Maybe some youngster did use long cartridges. But they're a hell of a lot more expensive.'

Higham sighed. 'For God's sake, Straun! You think that

would worry them? If they couldn't steal them off Dad they'd get them free off Social Security.'

'You think it was just a stray shot—no more?'

'I think someone just loosed off at a bird or something and hit this American by mistake. Realized what he'd done and made himself scarce.' Higham looked at me as though challenging me to say otherwise. Then, when I didn't say anything, 'What's the alternative? That someone murdered the man? Who, for God's sake? Segal had only been in the country for a couple of days, which is a short time to make enemies. And if one of his friends on the tour did it, why wait and do it here?'

'I don't know,' I said. I tried picturing Segal's last minutes. So the high velocity shot might have been an accident, but why had the Albatross been so anxious to look inside that house?

I repeated as much to the Superintendent but it didn't get me anywhere. 'Used to be a pub, you say? Well, he just wanted to have a look at it again. Nostalgia. What else?'

He had a point there, because whatever memories Albatross Segal had been conjuring up in those last few minutes of his life, they were gone for good. 'He probably drank there, between missions,' I said. I found it easy enough to go along with the idea. 'Just wanted to have a look at the old watering-hole once more.'

Superintendent Higham nodded. 'The Yanks won't make a fuss if they know it's an accident. Happens all the time over there.'

'It does?'

'You wouldn't believe it. I did a year exchange posting over there, and believe me, life's cheap. It's the frontier still. People kill each other in hunting accidents and it's just put down to an occupational hazard.'

I said, 'I'll bear it in mind.' If Americans were really as laid back as all that when it came to sudden death I couldn't imagine anyone asking why Segal's nostalgia should lead him out of what had obviously been the bar to an upstairs room. I asked it, but then it wasn't my business.

'You'll be seeing his friends, I suppose?' Higham asked.

'I suppose so.' I knew very well so, but it was something I'd been putting off.

Higham nodded. 'They'd appreciate it, I'm sure. But keep it light.'

I said, 'Their most distinguished senior member's been shot dead. It's hardly something you can play for laughs.'

'Well, let's say unofficial.'

Up till now I'd been getting on all right with Higham, but now I wasn't so sure. 'I'm on leave,' I said. 'And a long way from home.'

'Just thought I'd mention it.' Higham had the grace to look embarrassed. 'But we get a lot of American visitors in these parts, most of them war veterans. There are local associations for them—hospitality groups. We want to keep them happy.'

I nodded. It was his patch and it was up to him to run it any way he wanted. 'I'll try not to rock the boat.'

I gave them a statement and Higham stood me lunch at his local, where I ate steak and kidney pudding and very good, too. We parted with expressions of mutual esteem and a rather attractive WPC drove me home.

The cottage was empty when I got there, so I guessed that either the journey to Peterborough had taken longer than expected or Laurie had had to hang about waiting for Smith to finish his business in town. I missed her. Now that it was too late to do anything about it I wished I'd told Higham I was on holiday and taken Sam back to school myself. As is usual in these cases, remorse set in and I changed my clothes with a growing air of despondency. There were four or five shelves of books and I flipped idly through the first ones that came to hand. *The Forsyte Saga,*

Rogue Herries and a bound volume of something called *The Small Bore Rifle Quarterly*, which was interesting. Whose? *The Forsyte Saga* had 'Lucy Pinecoffin, 1954' scribbled on the flyleaf. Lucy Hayward née Pinecoffin, presumably. No fine old Cornish name on the rifle magazine, but the first one had a telephone number scribbled in pencil on the cover. *Butcher: Wen 2793*, and the writing was the same.

I dropped into a chair and thumbed through a few of the glossy pages of long-forgotten shooting competitions, descriptions of new rifles, advertisements, and letters complaining bitterly of this and that. Few things less interesting than other people's past enthusiasms. Maybe I could entertain myself for a while wondering if Lucy Hayward had shot Albatross Segal, but wondering was about as far as I was going to get. Oh, she had the skill all right, but then almost anyone who works the land can shoot. Come to that, the better the shot the less likelihood of someone getting hit accidentally, always providing it *was* accidentally.

The first bat of the evening flitted past the window. Why make trouble? as Superintendent Higham would say. Killers need a motive and it was going to need a pretty exotic flight of fancy to suggest why anyone should want to kill a complete stranger. I tossed *The Small Bore Quarterly* on to the bed and reached for *The Forsyte Saga*, conscious of the fact that I was a good deal more interested in Laurie's return than the troubles of Soames and the tiresome Irene. What was it that made rational men behave like fools when confronted with a certain kind of woman? I was, as many a man must have done before me, trying to put myself in Soames Forsyte's shoes when Saul Hayward's voice broke in on me from outside in the courtyard.

'Straun! Are you there?'

I went to the window. Hayward was standing there in his shirtsleeves, his fair hair glowing in the moonlight, clutching a bottle by the neck in one huge hand.

'I'm here,' I said without any great enthusiasm.

'Come and have a drink.'

I didn't want to go and have a drink with anyone, let alone with a host who'd apparently had several already. On the other hand, he had been hospitable and for that I was indebted. I reflected with a kind of gloomy satisfaction that this was the kind of thing one avoided by staying at hotels. It was some consolation to have it proved that I'd been right all along and I wished heartily that Laurie had been around to witness the fact.

'Well,' Hayward was saying with a touch of belligerence, 'are you coming to have this drink or aren't you?'

I nodded, as though this was the invitation I'd been waiting for all evening. 'Yes,' I said. 'Right now.'

I pulled on a jacket and went out. I guessed it was as dark now as it was likely to get, because the huge sky seemed never to be entirely without light, like summer nights in the far north. A couple of bats circled the house, usually creatures that I have few feelings for one way or the other, but now for some reason the harbingers of the curious unease that had been with me for the last couple of days. I told myself that this happened with the Fens: instant like or dislike. With myself, the latter. Oh well. I greeted Saul Hayward and he handed me a glass, an unexpected amenity.

'Nice night.'

'Yes.' I held the glass while he slopped whisky into it. 'When. Whoa!'

Apparently water didn't come with the deal. Hayward replenished his own glass and led the way to the paddock fence. Sensibly, the horse had gone to bed. Hayward stared at the empty half-acre of grass. 'How did you get on with the American?'

Odd the way different people react to tragedy. Albatross Segal was dead and it didn't matter a damn how I'd got on with him. I said a bit shortly, 'He struck me as a pleasant enough chap. It was miserable luck, what happened to him.'

'Interrupted his sentimental tour, you could say.'

It seemed an unnecessarily heartless comment, but drink takes all of us in different ways. I said, 'I don't know about sentimentality. Nostalgia, maybe. I gather the USAAF boys were pretty popular round here.'

'Woman. The invader's rightful spoil.' Hayward sipped at his drink and watched the dipping flight of the bats. 'You know that?'

'We were both fighting on the same side. Seems a bit hard to call them invaders.' Really, he was an impossible man.

'How's the sciatica?' I asked, heartlessly.

Hayward grunted. 'All right. Nothing much wrong with it at breakfast, as a matter of fact. Just had to get out of showing people around.' He remembered his manners. 'Sorry to have landed you with the job. You probably loathe them as much as I do.'

God preserve us the right to our prejudices. So far as I'm concerned, nobody should be under a legal obligation to love his neighbour and if Saul Hayward had a thing about Americans that was his business and not mine. 'As a matter of fact,' I said, 'I quite like them.'

'Has it ever occurred to you that American troops must have fathered literally *thousands* of children while they were over here?'

Well, yes, they probably had. For a moment I wondered if some lusty GI had put horns on Saul Hayward but of course he was too young for that. I said consolingly, 'Come to that, our own drunken and licentious soldiery must have populated half the globe.' What was supposed to make Americans so different? 'Girls have always had a weakness for uniforms. I wouldn't be surprised if some of the victims of the Norse raiders didn't rape pretty easily.'

Hayward frowned. 'The victims, as you call them, were chosen women. Chosen to found a nation.' He slopped whisky into my glass and replenished his own. He said, 'It's a thousand years since then. A thousand years of straight English stock, and yet we sat back and watched it being diluted by a mongrel race who were only here by invitation.'

I sipped my own drink and wondered what had set this off, bees in bonnet usually needing some kind of kick to get them moving. There was little point in reminding him that as a race we British had been diluted from day one, that a ceaseless tide of Romans, Norsemen, Normans, Jews, European refugees and just about every other race you might care to mention had lapped against our shores. Hayward's resentment of Americans was based on some personal kink that wasn't going to be shifted by anything as ordinary as logic. I said consolingly, 'Well, if you don't like them, ignore them. It's about all you can do these days.'

'There was a time when we'd have fought back.'

We? Then it struck me he was talking about the Saxons. Probably in his booze-fuzzed mind he imagined an ancestral Hereward looking down at him disapprovingly from some Saxon Valhalla, waiting for Americans to be harried through the fens as had been William's Normans all those years ago. I said, 'Even Hereward packed it in in the end.' At least, I supposed he did. Real history is as vague about Hereward as it is about Robin Hood.

Hayward frowned. I watched him staring at the ground, forcing himself to collect the thoughts he'd affectively numbed with alcohol. Finally he said almost petulantly, 'Of course he didn't pack it in, as you put it. He fought on. The year after Morcar and Siward were taken he took refuge at the house of a woman called Olwyn. She had lost her first husband at the sack of Peterborough, and in revenge she murdered Hereward by putting poison in his wine.'

I said, 'I hadn't heard that.' Well, not about Hereward but the essentials were pretty familiar. Odd what a thing we have about betrayers and the betrayed. Judas and Mordred and whoever the abbess was who was supposed to have poisoned Robin Hood. It stood to reason that a cult figure like Hereward couldn't have fallen in battle like any ordinary man, there had to be something unsporting about his death. Still, I was the last person to look a gift legend in the mouth, so I asked where the great man had been buried.

'Nobody knows. My guess is that it was round here somewhere but nobody knows exactly where. But his people saw him off in the old style. Boat burial.'

Well, they didn't come much more old-style than that. There had been a time when sea-rovering Norsemen had sent their dead leaders on their last journey aboard a burning longboat. Later, they no longer burnt the ship, but buried it on land beneath a huge funeral mound, a complete boat with its dead captain and his arms and most treasured possessions so that he'd have them ready to hand in the afterlife. Boat burial was a Bronze Age practice, though traces of it had lingered on through Roman times, usually with a ship-shaped outline of stones rather than a real vessel, which must have been something of a money-saver. I said mildly, 'I thought boat burials were a bit out of fashion by the eleventh century.'

For a moment I thought Hayward hadn't heard me, because he was staring out across the moonlit fen as though he expected a funeral boat to sail over it at any moment. His arms were hanging over the fence and the bottle of whisky he'd been clutching in his left hand slipped through his fingers and landed on the grass. About a fiver's worth of straight malt had cheered the local insect population before I grabbed it by the neck and refreshed my own glass.

'Splendid way to go,' Hayward said at last. He was obviously very drunk but not so that he had passed the reflective stage. 'For a man like Hereward, the only way to go.'

'Yes,' I said. 'I suppose so.' It was getting cold and I was bored by Hayward's drunken ramblings. I suppose something of that came through, because he gave me a baleful look and let go the fence.

'Come. Got something to show you.'

I should have said it was late and was past my bedtime but I didn't want to be unfriendly and the man had a certain lunatic authority, so I followed him as he went out of the garden and on to the perimeter track of the old airfield. At that time of night you didn't notice the crops, all you could see was the dark outline of the old huts and the concrete runway pale in the light of the moon. It didn't need all that much imagination to see oneself back in the war. I suppose we walked for about quarter of a mile before Hayward pulled up in front of a big hump of what looked like raised earth but what was really turf over concrete. There was a door, marked STRICTLY NO ENTRY with a big bar and a padlock.

Hayward said, 'This is it.' He took a key from his pocket, and a torch. I'd expected the lock to put up a fight but it opened easily enough. Inside, the light from his torch picked out a flight of steps that went down into the further dark.

'They used to arm the bombs in here,' Hayward said. He walked on down the steps and I followed him. It was cold and smelled of earth. It was like going into a tomb. Why had I been fool enough to come?

'You turn a bit right here.'

I turned a bit right and stopped. Hayward was playing the white beam of his torch round the underground cavern that had once housed the squadron's 1000-pounders. The walls were of concrete, like the floor, and the roof was semi-circular vaulted steel girders. But it wasn't the construction of the place that stopped me in my tracks, it was what filled the floor. Not bombs, they'd long gone. Instead, the place was filled with the ribs and strakes of a vast wooden boat. The thing was new built, still incomplete, the floor littered with shavings and woodworking tools, yet strangely familiar. The boat must have been all of forty or fifty feet long, shallow but immensely broad in the beam, with a great carved wooden prow that towered above me. The torchlight threw queer shadows on the whitewashed walls of the shelter and suddenly the penny dropped.

'It's a longship!' My voice sounded unnaturally loud in that cavern. 'Good God, man, you're building a Viking longship!'

'Beautiful, isn't she?' Hayward reached up and touched the planking above him. 'This is it, Straun. Mine, when it's time to go. In the old way. The last ship burial in Britain.'

CHAPTER 5

'Oh there you are!' Footsteps behind us, a woman's voice. Lucy Hayward, unsurprised, wearing a light weatherproof jacket and businesslike rubber boots. She looked at the two of us and addressed herself to Saul. 'It's getting late. And you wanted to have a look at Armstrong's account before you went to bed.'

'Did I? Yes, I suppose I did.' Hayward came back to rationality without apparent effort. Perhaps he was used to switching from planning his own funeral to sorting out a seed merchant's bill. Of the two, I suppose I was the one who was embarrassed.

Lucy turned her attention to me. 'I think I saw Mr Smith's car on the top road just now. The Land-Rover's still in front of the house if you want to pick Laurie up at the hangar.'

'That's kind of you.' And it was. I could have done without the dismissive bit but I understood it all right. Bad enough to have a stranger lifting up a family stone without having him hang around to have an extended peer underneath. I felt a sudden glimmer of the sad business of one half of a couple having a sadness and the other half loyally pretending it's not there. Usually it's sex but now and again something different. Well, a wealthy East Anglian farmer planning his own boat burial was at least different. Harmless, but different. I met Lucy Hayward's eyes but there is nothing quite so blank as the eyes of a woman who intends to tell you absolutely nothing.

I took the Land-Rover and drove down to the South Hangar, a curiously spooky business for one not given to that kind of fancy. There's an anonymity about driving in the dark, just what one can see in the headlights, the dials in front of you and that's it. Dusk in the fens is the time the place waits for. Dark dribbling across the endless fields, filling up the dykes, flooding the empty land. There aren't many people about during the day, but at dusk there are none. It there's anything living it's the odd homegoing skein of geese and whatever watches from the ditches and the shelter of twisted Arthur Rackham trees. Whatever ghosts haunt wartime airfields must get their kit together and get on parade at dusk. As I drove along the old perimeter track, past dispersal points laden with sugar beet, I could have sworn that over the Land-Rover's diesel clatter I could still hear the muffled thunder of those fifty-year-old engines.

Imagination makes cowards of us all. I remembered my mother's sister, no very fey lady, swearing that she could not with comfort stand within sight of the battlefield of Culloden. And there had been an old man, a friend of my father's, who swore that in India he had stood on the battlefields of Chilianwalla and watched the hundred-and-fifty-year-past battle fought again. If the right circumstances could conjure up those ancient guns, why not ancient aircraft? I put my foot down so as to make more noise and drive spectral sounds away.

It seemed a long way to the South Hangar. It *was* a long way, come to that, it being easy to overlook the fact that bomber runways tended to be the thick end of a mile, it taking all of that to lug tons of bombs off the ground in those pre-jet days. I concentrated on the present. No trouble. The South Hangar came up in the headlights, vast doors open. As I pulled up I could see the huge bulk of the B-24 reflecting the hangar lights. One Pratt and Whitney radial coughed and died, the props waggled a moment against compression, then froze, and I got out into the sweet burnt smell of aircraft exhaust.

'Hi!' Well, if you own an American World War Two

bomber, what else? Patrick Smith emerged from the cockpit in most inappropriate good suiting, followed by Laurie, likewise.

I said, 'Hello,' reminding me of some Waugh-like charac-ter who badly wanted to say 'Cheers' matily over a drink but couldn't quite bring himself to do it.

I was glad there'd been nobody in the Land-Rover to hear me carrying on about ghostly engines. If you're going to fantasize, do it in private. I stood up straight, an uncom-plicated, down-to-earth chap.

Smith said, 'I was just showing off my wares to Laurie here. She wanted to make sure they worked.'

Laurie here was sitting on a packing case looking suitably gratified, as well she might, it not being every girl who can command 1200 antique brake horse-power just like that.

I said, 'Everything go all right?'

'Everything went fine.' She was looking at me and smil-ing, so there wasn't any reason to think I'd said the wrong thing. She said, 'Sam spent the time getting a crash course on restoring aircraft. It's his new thing. If I'd been Patrick I'd have chucked him out of the car.'

So it was Patrick now, was it? The small green glowing lamp. And bloody silly anyway, considering that they'd been cooped up in a car together all day listening to my son rabbiting on. Of course she called him Patrick.

I said to him, 'You should have shut him up. Sam's enthusiasms tend to take over. Especially new ones.'

'Why not? At least he asks sensible questions.' An organ-ized character, this Patrick Smith, well able to appreciate that yours truly had had a day that had taken the fine edge off my temper. Not sufficiently involved to want to exploit the fact but not averse to observing Laurie and me at close quarters. After a day with her he was probably curious to discover what kind of man she went around with.

I said, 'It's no wonder. When Sam saw this place it must

have been like having one of his Airfix models come to life.'
And in a way it was. Possibly the sharp smell of undigested
aviation fuel that still lingered had something to do with it
but in its present surroundings the B-24 was incredibly
evocative of all the things one had read about fliers and
World War Two. The old Liberator wasn't beautiful in the
way that a Spitfire is beautiful. Judged purely on æsthetics
it was a great, slab-sided lump of a thing, squatting there
on huge tyred wheels. I was no expert but I couldn't help
feeling that Smith must have got the plane looking almost
exactly as she had when operational. Four Browning guns
projected through the perspex of the Boulton and Paul rear
turret and I guessed that getting hold of those must have
posed quite a few problems on their own. The metal cover-
ing of fuselage and wings had been painted the kind of dark
green one associates with bombers, and it had the faintly
scruffy look that working aircraft would have had. Just
below the pilot's cabin someone had painted a big-breasted
young woman standing on a plinth and holding aloft a
torch. Together with her *Liberty Belle* logo she made a pretty
good example of early pop art, helped out by the outlines
of a dozen or so miniature bombs just to the right of her. I
nodded up at them. 'Do you know if this one really was
operational?'

Smith looked up at the scoreboard too. 'Oh, that's genuine all right. Fourteen ops. We checked pretty carefully.'

'Where did you find her?'

Laurie said, 'That was the first thing Sam wanted to
know. They found her behind a pub about ten miles from
here.'

'You're joking.' I didn't doubt her for a moment since
that was presumably what Smith had told her, but the
statement called for some polite disbelief.

'Most of it was in a barn,' Smith said. 'The wings
were outside, but by and large the thing was complete.

Apparently the last landlord but one had been a Liberator
buff and somehow managed to buy one off the Yanks at the
end of the war.'

'Just like that?'

'Well, nobody wanted the things. The US government
parked God knows how many aircraft in the Nevada desert
or somewhere and just left them to rot. Some they cut up,
but the Yanks were never great on salvage.' Smith reached
up and touched the undercarriage strut behind him. An
oddly appealing gesture, like a man fumbling the ear of a
well-loved dog. I wondered how many man hours had gone
into restoring that huge chunk of machinery.

I said, 'How many of these are left?' I had an idea that
there was only one Lancaster still airworthy but for all I
knew Liberators were two a penny.

'A few in the States,' Smith said. 'And this one here.
They built something over 19,000 during the war and that's
all we've got to show for it.'

I said, 'So far as you're concerned, I'd say you had quite
a lot to show for it.'

'Yes, I suppose so.' Smith considered. 'Hard to cost out.
Money, of course. And three years' work for four men.' He
went over to a big industrial space heater and switched it
on. The thing started with a woof and hot air spilled over
us like a warm blanket. Money, he'd said. That gadget
alone must have cost hundreds of pounds. I looked round
the hangar at the accumulated gear. The place was like a
machine shop and one didn't have to be a cost accountant
to see that nothing had been skimped. I wondered where
the money had come from.

I said tentatively, 'Are the four of you in this together?'
It was meant to be a nice way of asking who paid the bills
but I suppose not nice enough.

'Jack Keating's an aeronautical engineer. Toby Whitton's a mathematician but a sort of machinist manqué,

Frank McInroe's nominally a draughtsman but in reality is a natural born mechanic.' Smith numbered them off on his fingers. 'I pay them peanuts compared to what they could earn elsewhere. They live pretty uncomfortably in what used to be the old flight offices and they work all hours of the day and night. For why?'

'I don't know,' I said. 'Tell me.'

He shrugged his shoulders. 'I've never asked them in so many words. But presumably they're like me. They just like messing about with old aircraft.'

England is supposed to be the home of eccentrics, the last bastion of those who want to do their own thing. To be a notable eccentric, it helps if you have money. Apparently Smith had. I asked, 'When you finally get it to fly, what do you do with it?'

Smith considered. 'A good question. As a matter of fact this one flies fine already, legally certificated, safe as houses. I may sell it to a chap in California called Haas who's been after it for some time. But not till after the Michiner Field Expo next month. No way.'

Laurie explained for my benefit. 'Patrick was telling us about it this morning. It's in Georgia. A grand sort of get-together for World War Two aircraft. People are flying in from all over the world.' She sounded as though she wished she was going to be there. I felt a twinge of unease. In all our time together she'd never summoned up this amount of enthusiasm for police work. What kind of two-hour chat turned a hard-nosed literary agent into a vintage aircraft nut? I didn't know the answer and I was by no means sure I wanted to.

'You're flying the Atlantic?' Obviously. How in God's name was he going to get to the southern United States otherwise? I wondered how much longer I anticipated standing around making fatuous comments. I tried qualifying things. 'I didn't know B-24s had that much range.'

'Most of them didn't.' Smith looked faintly surprised at getting a sensible comment. 'As a matter of fact the early ones were shipped over in bloody great crates. Took time and used a lot of shipping. Then from the end of 1941 Consolidated brought out the long-range version with extra tanks in the wing bays. The RAF called it a Mark V rather than a B-24D and used it for anti-submarine work and Atlantic patrolling. Plenty of range. *Liberty Belle*'s a Mark V.'

I liked to think that if I'd rebuilt an aircraft I'd have the confidence to fly the Atlantic in it but I knew I wouldn't. I hated flying three thousand miles over that cold ocean in a big modern jet, let alone a clapped-out old bomber. And crew. I asked Smith about the crew. 'You're taking your own people?'

'Only Keating as navigator. The others will be Americans.' For a moment Smith looked embarrassed, not so much at my question as by his answer. Then he said, 'Politics. Money. A dull old world it would be without them.'

Well, ground staff and aircrew were traditionally two sides of the coin. I asked, 'So how many would it have taken to fly a B-24 in wartime?'

Smith waggled his hands. 'Varied with the job, but ten was usual with the USAAF. A couple of pilots, radio op, navigator, bombardier and five turret gunners. Obviously we can manage on a lot less than that, but the Yanks have a thing about the B-24. I could sell the crew space half a dozen times if I wanted to.'

'Why not?' Why not indeed. On things like round the world yacht races it happened all the time.

Smith smiled. 'Why not indeed? Actually, it doesn't work out quite like that. The old *Belle* gets a certain amount of sponsored help from American servicemen over here and they decide who gets a place. They're all air crew, of course. I pick 'em up at West Canby.'

'Where's that?'

'Cambridgeshire—about seventy miles from here. It's a pretty big American base and I gather they're planning to give us a good send-off.' Smith paused. 'After that the old plane's got her long hop home. A broken hop, anyway. West Canby to Shannon. Shannon to Gander, Newfoundland. After that I'm not sure. There's some talk of putting down at New York or New Jersey before heading down south. We'll know more when the time comes.'

I looked up at *Liberty Belle* and tried to imagine heading her out over the cold grey Atlantic with her fifty-year-old engines thrashing alongside of me, knowing that I'd virtually put the whole thing together and that if anything went wrong it would be my own fault. The instinctive reaction of the non-technical man busily washing his hands of the whole thing. Nonsense, of course, because a true craftsman will rely on his own work in preference to that of others. I wondered where Smith had acquired his expertise.

Come to that, I wondered what his friends were doing. Drinking in the *Packet Boat* or playing Scrabble in the one-time airmen's quarters? It had to be one or the other, because Wendal Fen wasn't exactly rich in alternatives.

Laurie stood up. 'Time we were going.' Women have a built-in meter to tell them just that. They may ignore it, but at least they know without being told. The hint given, I too could see that Smith was waiting for something. Or someone. Laurie was saying, 'Thanks again for the ride, Patrick. From me and Sam too.'

'Any time.' Smith paused and listened. From the direction of the main entrance a vehicle was approaching rapidly, but whatever he'd been waiting for I was pretty sure it wasn't this, because he was as surprised as we were.

I said, 'Visitors?'

'It would appear so.' He didn't move from where he stood by the aircraft but his eyes were on the entrance to the hangar. Whatever the vehicle was stopped just out of sight and someone in a Barbour jacket and soaking jeans came into the floodlights. I recognized one of Smith's team. Tall and thin, red-haired, with the kind of anguished face that seems the prerogative of a certain kind of academic. Frank McInroe?

He looked at Smith, then noticed us, then looked back again. 'I think you'd better come.'

Smith hesitated for a decision-making second, probably cursing his luck that he hadn't got rid of us five minutes before. But clearly he was stuck with us.

He said, 'Take it easy, Frank. What is it?'

'Toby's dead.'

The words hung about in that huge echo chamber of a hangar, McInroe looked sick and a bit scared, Smith oddly unmoved, but then it takes us all different ways. Toby? I remembered another of Smith's team members as Jack Keating. Which left—yes, Whitton, presumably Toby. Smith said, 'What happened?'

'We found him. Drowned.' Then, 'We did our best with him but it was too late.'

'I'll come.' Smith looked at me. 'You're a policeman. Perhaps you'd better come too.' An authoritative note I hadn't noticed before.

I nodded. I was curious about McInroe saying that they'd found Whitton drowned. People who die that way don't usually surface for some time. How long had he been missing? And drowned in what, for God's sake? But McInroe looked ragged enough as it was without pushing him, and anyway I'd find out soon enough.

We went outside, where McInroe had left an old American army jeep, not roomy.

I said, 'You take that. I'll follow.' Then to Laurie, 'Not you.'

Why does learning come so hard to some people? I'm

reasonably bright in some ways, dishearteningly thick in others. The 'not you' bit to someone like Laurie was asking for trouble.

She said, 'You don't have to cosset me, for God's sake. I don't particularly want to look, but you'll need the Land-Rover. And it's a long way to walk home.'

'The keys are still in my station wagon.' Patrick Smith remembered the extra vehicle, which was more than I had. 'Take it, and I'll pick it up in the morning.'

Laurie said meekly, 'All right. Thanks.'

A logical solution to a pretty trivial problem, no reason to be put out. But I resented that meekness. Laurie, my love, you have never been meek with me. Why so with a restorer of ancient aircraft? And why was I fretting about this and that when a man lay dead?

I said, 'Thanks, Patrick. We'd better get going. You lead the way.'

We went outside and got into the cars.

It wasn't all that far. A couple of miles perhaps as the jeep bumps. If you're following the vehicle ahead at night in strange country it's a full-time job and you live in the white arc cast by your headlights and to hell with what goes on in the dark on either side of you. The Land-Rover was open and I could smell the cold, damp smell of reeds and mud, not on in a landscape of pencil-straight, dredged-out rivers and oversize drains. The red lamps in front swung right and stopped. I pulled up alongside the jeep and got out as Smith came over.

'Where are we?'

'Wendal Fen.' He nodded out over the rushes and I could see that we were beside an open stretch of black water that lay flat as glass under the faint light of the new moon. So this was the undrained fen Hayward had told me about. A breath of wind stirred the rushes and spread ripples over the surface of the fen and an ungainly, long-legged bird rose with a clatter almost at our feet and flapped slowly off to some safer spot on our right. Seen in daylight, the fen must have been a birdwatcher's paradise, miles from anywhere and a home from home for waterfowl of every kind. At night it was an uncomfortable place, a kind of last glimpse of the way the country had been a thousand years ago, before man learned how to drain the fens. In Hereward's day, such stretches of marshy water would have covered most of the land, broken up by little islands of dry land here and there where the fenlanders lived. At night, without planes or power cables to clutter up the landscape it was pretty easy to imagine oneself back in that water world of Saxon times. It was a chill and unfriendly place and I felt its antagonism as a personal thing.

I looked at McInroe. 'Where?'

It's extraordinarily easy to get disorientated in the dark. We followed him, stumbling through ankle-deep mud with reeds crackling under our feet as we passed. Eventually we came out into a clearing where there was an elementary kind of mooring, with a couple of big fibreglass dories tied up to iron stakes driven deep in the mud. In front of them the short, broad-shouldered member of Smith's team, crouching beside the still dark shape of a human body. I did a quick bit of elimination. The chap looking up at us would be Keating.

We bent over the shape on the ground, the human remains of Toby Whitton. He was dressed in a frogman's wetsuit but with no masks or air tanks and in the half light his face was blue and lifeless.

I said, 'Where was he when you found him?' I was giving Whitton a quick going-over but he must have been long past any kind of help.

Keating nodded to the north. 'In the rushes, up there.' He looked at Smith.

'Well?'

'He'd been diving and I thought he'd been at it a long time. Then I heard a noise like someone coming ashore over there so I went to have a look. Toby was lying face down in the mud. His mask was off and lying beside him, so I called Frank and we did what we could to get the water out of him. We tried resuscitation but it wasn't any good. So I got in the jeep and came and fetched you.'

Smith said, 'Take him back to the cars.' Then he remembered and looked at me. 'OK by you?'

'Yes,' I said. 'Take him back.' McInroe and Keating got busy, surprisingly efficient when one considered that they hadn't done it before. To Smith I said, 'All right. Now what were they doing here?'

He looked at me, possibly wondering if he could get rid of me without answering questions, and decided no. Finally he said, 'You've heard the local legend, I suppose?'

'Tell me,' I said.

'About the B-24 back in 1943.'

'No,' I said. 'I haven't heard about that.'

'Seems that there was this aircraft that never got properly airborne.' Smith paused and I got the impression that whatever the story was, he believed it.

'She'd just got her wheels up when the engines cut or something and the whole lot just went into the fen.'

I remembered Hayward saying something about a lost plane. 'Did they ever find out what had gone wrong?'

Smith shrugged his shoulders. 'They never got her out. I suppose they had better things to do in those days, and anyway the thing would have been sucked down like a brick —after all, a Lib weighs about twenty-five tons. It sounds a bit cold-blooded, but then, aircraft were coming down in the drink pretty regularly and, like they say, there was a war on. But there's not a war on now, so we decided to get the old girl up.'

I said, 'I'm surprised nobody's tried before.'

'They probably would have done, only most of the people who put up money for that kind of thing want proof that there's a plane down there, and all we've got is a kind of local legend. In my experience, legends of that sort generally turn out to be pretty well based on fact.' Smith looked morosely at the figure lying on the ground. 'Only just now it doesn't seem much in exchange for Toby's life.'

Well no, it didn't. I said, 'Wouldn't it be safer to do this kind of thing in daylight?'

'Much safer,' Smith agreed. 'But daylight work's not on. Someone would be bound to see us.'

'Would that matter? Salvaging a smashed plane isn't illegal.'

Smith said, 'This one is.'

'Why this one?'

Some kind of large water bird hit the surface of the fen and gave a brief, petulant clap of wings, but nobody paid him any attention.

Smith said, 'This one's illegal because what's left of the crew must still be in it.'

CHAPTER 6

In the fens the dawn spills out over the edge of the flat land and the light is reflected down from the huge sky. It wakes people early, and no wonder. It woke me early, and I'd rather have slept. Not having the option, I lay awake in my chaste bed, restless and ill at ease. Morning does not banish as of right the nonsenses of the night before, pillow talk carried on discreetly from a sitting position on the edge of Laurie's bed. Discretion quite unnecessary, since Sam was now safely back at school and unlikely to be corrupted by his father's sex life, but that sort of evening just the same.

It had been late by the time we'd got back to the cottage, what with waiting while Sergeant Devenish drove himself the fifteen or so miles from his base at Easterham, then waiting again for the ambulance from somewhere marginally closer which eventually took Toby Whitton's body away. Sergeant Frederick Devenish had turned out to be a large, methodical and essentially well-meaning chap of the kind I'd imagined had long gone out of business. He had been impressed by a London copper, taken careful statements, done everything by the book. If he thought it odd that he should have me as a customer twice in three days he didn't let on.

Back at the cottage Laurie had said, 'You didn't tell him that the crew were still in that plane. Neither did Patrick.' Well, she'd had a point there. Smith had simply said that Keating, Whitton and McInroe had been trying to locate the wreck of an aircraft and Sergeant Fred hadn't got around to asking why all this had taken place at night. He'd asked me how I'd got to be on the scene and I'd told him, end of story.

To Laurie, I'd said, 'No, we didn't.'

'Why not? Why didn't Patrick?'

I'd said, 'Presumably because he's aware that for some time now it's been illegal to attempt the salvage of crashed aircraft if there's reason to believe they still have the bodies of their crew aboard.'

She'd looked at me a bit blankly. 'For God's sake, Angus, you're a policeman! You can't just stand there and pretend something isn't happening.'

At which point I'd said foolishly that I'd imagined she'd have approved of my stretching a point on Patrick's behalf as she so clearly enjoyed his company. It was a damn silly thing to say but how readily do we hurl ourselves into the pit which we have dug.

'If you don't like being a policeman why don't you give it up and take your writing seriously instead?' It was a familiar theme and one to which Laurie would always return, given half a chance.

'I do like being a bloody policeman.' I liked writing too, and so far I'd managed to combine both with reasonable success. Must a man sacrifice half of himself just to satisfy a literary agent's ego?

'Then why—'

'Because Smith doesn't *know* there's a plane down there, he just thinks there is.' I paused to let that sink in. Then I went on, 'Look, there's obviously some kind of local folklore that says a B-24 went into the fen during the war and was never found. One of those things everyone has heard about but nobody actually saw. Apparently the incident doesn't tie up with planes officially listed as missing. But it's a bit late in the day to check. In any case, nobody seems to know exactly when the accident occurred, or even the names of the crew. All you get is that it happened. Sometime. Personally I think Smith's let his enthusiasm run away with him. If you get hooked on something strongly enough you'll believe what you want to believe.'

'Patrick's perfectly rational.'

'Patrick obviously made a deep impression.' I could hear myself saying that particular nonsense and it sounded like another person talking. What the hell was wrong with me? What was wrong with the two of us, for that matter?

Laurie had frowned. Had she turned on me it would have been no more than I deserved but the look of boredom was dangerous. 'For God's sake, Angus, I'm tired, if you're not. Just go to bed.'

'If you wish.' Pompous to the last.

I'd gone to bed and slept badly, conscious of having made a fool of myself and uncertain why. I was not normally bloody-minded. It was a relief when the light filtering in between the curtains grew strong enough to justify getting up and dressed. Round about eight I knocked on Laurie's door.

'Come in.'

I went in and made appropriate noises. She was up and dressed too, looking rather county in a check wool skirt with a cashmere cardigan over a rollneck sweater, the always fascinating ability of women to adjust themselves to their surroundings. I'd expected to suffer for my shortcomings, but no.

'Do you think it's going to be a decent day?'

'Possibly.' I hadn't given the matter a thought, nor did I now, for that matter. She was sitting with her back to me at the kind of dressing-table that's kidney-shaped and cluttered with triple mirrors, an unfamiliar setting for some-one who didn't make a thing of being feminine. I put my hands on her shoulders unrebuked and saw that she was looking at me out of the centre mirror. I met the reflected look, feeling relief that we were apparently back on an even keel, and no hard feelings.

She said amiably, 'It could be raining for all you know.'

I glanced out of the window. No rain, a pale blue sky clear of cloud. 'No,' I told her, 'not raining.'

Laurie smiled. 'Good. You know, I rather like it here.'

Well, that had been pretty clear from the beginning. With singular lack of finesse I said, 'I don't. I hate the bloody place.'

'Well, go then.'

I said, 'I can't very well until the car's ready.'

'No, I suppose not.' Laurie was good at being unruffled, and her reflection smiled at me. 'Never mind. Aren't you playing golf today?'

'Hayward's taking me over to his club,' I told her. 'It'll give me chance to meet Segal's friends.'

'Doesn't it seem a bit heartless, playing golf when that poor man has been killed?'

'Yes,' I agreed, 'it does. But I've got a feeling his friends will be playing regardless, which is probably what he would have liked. After all, he must have risked his neck often enough in these parts, and back in the war you didn't drop everything just because one of your friends got killed. Even accidentally.'

'Do you honestly believe that?'

'I don't know,' I confessed. 'It's the way they behaved in *Dawn Patrol* but goodness knows if they ever did it for real.' A feeling of resentment, not for the first time, against being born too late for me to know for myself what it had been like. I added, 'Also, I'm hoping for nine holes with Bob Bannerman today. I know it's self-indulgence but it's something I'd hate to miss.'

'Don't expect too much, lover. People change.'

'Yes,' I said. 'I'd noticed.'

She fiddled with something on the dressing-table. 'Your Albatross friend. Are you quite sure it was an accident?'

'I don't have to be sure,' I said. 'That's the coroner's worry.'

'I know, but you haven't answered my question.'

I said, 'Damn it, I'm not *sure*. But he was among strangers, in a strange country. Who'd want to murder the man? What motive could there be? Quite apart from the fact that people aren't usually assassinated with a .22 rabbit rifle.' I paused. 'What makes you ask?'

'You're broody. Lucy Hayward has a .22.'

'I know,' I said. 'It's likely that lots of people have round here. And she said she was in her kitchen when she heard the shot.'

'You questioned her?'

'No,' I said. 'It's not my case. She just said that in passing.'

She nodded, as though she'd cleared something up. 'You'll unwind with a little golf. You always do.'

'Are you coming?'

I thought that for a moment she'd hesitated, but I could have been mistaken because her voice was casual as she said, 'Of course. I'd love to see your Mr Bannerman. And in any case, what should I do here?'

Something came to mind, but this time I had the sense not to say it out loud.

Steeple Thurston, Saul Hayward's club, turned out to be about fifteen miles away on the Wisbech road.

Hayward was due to do the driving in his Land-Rover, an arrangement for which I hadn't much enthusiasm. Still, there was no alternative and after all, I'd been running around in one of his farm vehicles and sleeping in the man's bed. Nevertheless, the prospect of his presence didn't exactly lighten my day.

Out of our host's hearing, Laurie said, 'You might at

least try to *look* pleased. What's wrong with the poor man, anyway?'

'Nothing, apart from the fact he's barking mad.'

'I thought he was rather hospitable. We'd have been sunk without him.'

I said, 'Yes, I know. But that doesn't mean he's not potty.' Not for the first time I marvelled at woman's capacity to latch on to people and ignore everything else. In the past forty-eight hours two people had died from unnatural causes which, while not sinister, was at least unusual. But because Hayward was hospitable and Patrick Smith absolutely fascinating the whole thing was a roaring success.

I suppose I'd rather hoped Saul would produce some outrageous bit of pro-Saxon dottiness over breakfast, but perhaps it was just the moon got him or something because be couldn't have been more normal. A certain amount of anti-American prejudice lingered, but no more. Lucy bade us farewell.

'I hope you have a wonderful day. Don't let Saul get you into trouble.'

'I'll take care, Mrs Hayward.' A bright smile, just to show that we all knew she was joking, but looking into those friendly eyes I wasn't sure.

Steeple Thurston turned out to be a slightly larger version of Wendal, an even longer single street of undistinguished houses, drab shops and forlorn business enterprises, an even stronger sense of a community struggling against its environment without notable success. The approach to the golf club was up a cheerless little lane beyond the last of the place's three pubs, jolting over unfilled potholes as one headed for a strip of trees bent permanently east to west by the prevailing wind. One gained access to the strip by way of a five-barred gate. Once through it one became aware of a car park, neatly done over with grey granite chips, and a generous scattering of new Range-Rovers, Bentley Turbos, Jaguars and big Mercs. A hard land, but apparently the rewards weren't all that bad.

Saul Hayward said, 'Nice little club.'

How right he was. It would have been a nice little club anywhere; in Steeple Thurston it was a kind of Shangri-La, gained after all that climbing through the snowy mountains. Set low, there were a lot more trees than were apparent from the village. The immaculate nineteen-thirties clubhouse, all pantiles and clapboard, looked out over the kind of super lawned fairways usually found only in stockbroker country. Someone had planted rhododendrons between the trees and the sand in the bunkers was almost white. Play Steeple Thurston at the right time of the year and you'd got yourself a kind of toy Augusta.

Saul Hayward must have been watching my face, because he said, 'You'll play on worse courses before you're my age.'

I did my best to sound appreciative, which wasn't difficult because you can tell a course that's deep down good without much trouble. This one had greenkeepers who knew their job and a committee who didn't hold back on the pennies. Also, just looking up the first fairway gave one a feeling that it was a course designed and run for people who wanted to play golf and not sit around the bar chewing over their balance sheets.

I said, 'This one's a well kept secret. How long's it been going?'

'Since the early 'thirties,' Hayward told me. 'Precious little money around here then. Place relied on the odd wealthy president to keep it going. But for the last twenty years or so things have looked up. Looked up quite a bit, as a matter of fact.'

'So I noticed, coming through the car park.'

Hayward nodded. 'There's a fair amount of money among members today. I must say, everyone tries to do his bit.' He broke off abruptly as the small terrace in front of the clubhouse began to fill up with well-turned-out men of late middle age who had to be Americans. I sensed Hayward curl up. 'You'll be wanting to have a word with those people, I imagine. We'll get together later.'

It would be an exaggeration to say that a man as big as Saul Hayward scuttled off, but he certainly left abruptly. Laurie watched him go with something like bewilderment. 'What on earth's come over him?'

'I imagine,' I said, 'that by "those people" he means the Americans. He can't stand them.'

'Why on earth not?'

'My dear girl, I don't know.' The sudden irritation one feels about having to explain something irrational. I thought she'd known. 'Maybe he caught Lucy out with a Yank or something.'

I went over and said hello to the dreaded Transatlantic cousins, about a dozen of them. Like all of their race, they were extra-ordinarily easy to meet, a people who get names right first time and have few difficulties when it comes to personal communication.

'Great to meet you, Angus. Tell us what we can do about Al.'

Strange how they could all have been cousins of Segal, even though a couple of them were black. I gathered that this particular golf society went by the name of the Real Estaters, of Landerville, Ohio. Their top man looked like Colonel Sanders without his beard but a hard man to buy a house off, none the less.

'Not a great deal, I'm afraid.' I cut that one short to introduce Laurie, which took some time. They must all have been between fifty and sixty but they did her self-esteem a power of good. When there was a chance, I said,

'It's in the hands of the local police, and of course there'll have to be an inquest. But I can't see them finding it anything but an accident.'

'Sure, it happens all the time.' It appeared that his name was O'Mara and by rights he should have been located somewhere in Manhattan. How had he strayed from Costello's to Landerville without losing that St Patrick's Day brogue? He said, 'You and your lady will be taking a drink now?'

It was half past ten of a fine morning and there didn't seem any reason why not, but I said tentatively, 'We wouldn't want to hold you up.'

'It's only among ourselves and the tee's booked for eleven.'

We repaired to the bar. With a drink in my hand I asked O'Mara why Segal had come to Wendal Fen alone.

'We thought he'd enjoy it more.'

'More than what?'

'More than with us.' O'Mara was a huge man who'd have looked all right building dams but must have seemed distinctly out of place flogging ranch-style homes. 'Don't let's fool ourselves, Inspector. We're none of us chickens, but Al was the only member of our society who was old enough to have actually fought in the war, so it's not as if we're a party of vets come here for a last look round. That's why we laid it on for Al to make the trip to his old base on his own. We'd have just kind of got in the way of his memories.'

'*You* laid his visit on?'

O'Mara nodded. 'Sure. We all knew about what he'd done in the war, same as we knew about him playing that great round of golf. Al Segal was a pretty well known character where we come from. But he wasn't after talking about himself, you'll understand. He was one hell of a fine real estate agent, but a quiet man.'

I nodded. 'And there weren't any other members of your society visiting old airfields or anything like that?'

'No, sir.' O'Mara looked puzzled. 'Like I said, all the guys in this society are in real estate. It's a real estate golf society. If that's not your business you don't get in. There are some real good organizations who look after World War Two stuff.'

'Then why did you come to Steeple Thurston? Was that Segal's idea?'

'Hell—he didn't even know we'd got it on our itinerary!' O'Mara spoke as though he meant it and there was a good deal of supporting rhubarbs from his listening friends. 'Primarily we came here because we'd never played your eastern courses before. And because the local hotels round here gave us a good deal.' He went on, 'Like I said, we all knew about Al shooting his albatross with the local champ back in the war. So we fixed it so we should play this particular course without Al knowing. Kind of a surprise. The secretary here's a nice guy who went along with the whole thing. Except the visit to the old airfield. We found out about that from the Allied Air Vets Association in Cambridge. You heard of them?'

I shook my head. 'No.'

'Mostly they fix tours, but they get the records and they know what's left to see of the old bases. Real nice people, too.'

He paused and we looked at each other. As usual, I'd ended a confrontation with an American feeling that I should have done better. I said, 'Well, I can't see any great problems at the inquest. In fact, it's a hundred to one the finding will be accidental death. After that the body is released to his next of kin. Is his wife still alive?'

O'Mara said cautiously, 'Al was divorced. Didn't have any children, so far as I know.' He paused. 'That make any problems?'

I said, 'I'm just a policeman on holiday. The locals will fill you in, but I imagine they'll drop this one in the lap of your Embassy in London.' I looked round the Real Estaters. They were looking suitably solemn but I got the impression that nobody was exactly heartbroken about Albatross Segal's demise. And why should they be? He wasn't anyone's close relative, or even distant, come to that. He was just someone they'd known in business, drank with occasionally, played golf with two or three times a year. Wasn't it Texas where more people were killed every year by gunshot than died on the roads? Looking at their faces, it struck me for the first time that what Americans had in common more than an accent and a love of Uncle Sam was an acceptance of mortality that one might have expected to have vanished with the Old West, but hadn't. These fairly ordinary business men weren't caught unawares by death. He hadn't surprised them carrying off their friend Segal. No sir! If you got to go, you got to go.

O'Mara said, 'I guess that's what embassies are paid for. Still, it's kind of nice that Al had a chance to meet the old champ again before he went.'

I liked the 'before he went' bit. I said, 'Yes, it is. But I shouldn't imagine either knew the other from Adam.'

'They were knowing each other like it was yesterday.' O'Mara gave a pleased smile. 'No change at all, they said.' He looked at me. 'They say you were knowing Bob Bannerman, too. You'll see.'

They took me in to meet Bob Bannerman. It was his club, God help us, but they'd taken him over in their amiable way, he being a bit of history and no mean charmer in his own right. He was sitting in the bar having a fortifying early something, looking pretty good for his eighty and whatever years. Old golfers, never having to grow themselves prodigious amounts of muscle, tend to age fairly gracefully. Also, they are rarely forced to give up the game entirely as they grow old, unlike weight-lifters and the rest. Golf is a game for life.

'You remember this feller, Bob? Angus Straun? Claims to have played with you way back.' Oh dear, did they have to? I wondered where the hell Saul Hayward was hiding. Maybe he didn't like Americans but he didn't have to abandon me to this kind of fate. I cringed with embarrassment, madly British.

'Och, the boy wonder!' Bannerman swivelled himself round on his bar stool, and it was true all right. There he was, the old schoolboy idol, not really changed a bit. He'd got the kind of lean, weatherworn face, thin-lipped, hook-nosed, that doesn't really change much with time. A bit stringier, higher coloured round the cheekbones, but that was about all. Cashmere sweater and Italian slacks spoke of money from the good days safely salted. Quite ridiculous that I should still feel this sense of awe. Or such gratification that he should remember me.

I said, 'Not such a boy any more.' I wondered why, fleetingly, I resented the presence of Laurie behind me, but then going back twenty years is a chastening experience, not one to be shared. I introduced her and the old boy regarded her with approval.

'Does this man of yours still play golf?' He pronounced it 'goff'.

'I know he's going to be very upset if he doesn't play a round with you today, Mr Bannerman.'

'Och, I don't play worth a damn any more,' my hero informed her. 'Handicap nine. Double figures any moment now.'

Laurie said, 'Angus plays to nine too. You'll play level. That's nice.'

'Away with you, girl. The last we played he was off plus one. In a daft tournament flogging some kind of bottled cat's piss, if you'll forgive the freedom of an old man's tongue.'

'It was Spanish gin,' I reminded him.

'Like I said. Some kind—' He broke off discreetly. 'If I remember aright, you beat me three and two.'

'I was lucky.'

'You were young, boy.'

'Yes.' It hadn't been my youth as much as his age, well past sixty. Even five years earlier and he'd have murdered me.

Bannerman said diffidently, 'I'm sorry about yon Segal. A nasty thing to have happened. Perhaps ye'd rather not play?'

I looked at the Real Estate golfers. If not his friends, they'd been his golfing cronies and, as I'd suspected, they were certainly not going to miss a round. 'No,' I said. 'Of course I'll play.'

Funny pulling on my studded shoes beside him in the locker-room again, talking the kind of trivia reserved for such occasions, the weather, the recurring hook or whatever. On the first tee I had a nasty moment when I thought the Americans were going to come round with us as a kind of gallery but I suspected they just wanted to see us on our way before getting about their own business. There were no caddies, of course, but Bannerman carried what looked like a half set of Pings on an electric-powered trolley. O'Mara, unasked, had put my bag on a similar machine.

'That's kind of you,' I said. 'Thanks.' The truth was that I'm a bag carrier by inclination, having little use for trolleys one pulls, let alone the power-driven type. Still, a kind thought and difficult to say no. I persuaded Bannerman that it was his honour and stood back and watched. Swings come and go, but swings of the type fashioned by Bob Bannerman seemed to be pretty permanent. He had never been one for messing about and I saw that he wasn't now.

The old boy simply took a three wood out of his bag, teed
his ball up and hit it. His swing was so effortless, so decep-
tively lazy, that it left one wondering at what point he
picked up the power that was driving the wretched ball
well over two hundred yards in a lovely controlled fade. I
watched awestruck, because at the age of eighty he didn't
seem to have lost a thing. Well, maybe a certain amount of
distance, but what was the odd twenty or thirty yards when
his drive had left the ball sitting up bang in the middle of
the fairway, a comfortable eight iron shot from the green?
The Americans must have thought the same because there
was a sudden patter of applause.

As I started for the tee Laurie caught at my arm.

'What is it?' Even if you don't know it already the books
will all tell you that what matters most in golf is concentration.

'If you lose on purpose he'll never forgive you.'

I said, 'I'll try to remember.' Did she really think I'd
insult the man by doing that? Really, there are times when
one wonders about the sanity of even those closest to you.
I took a driver and slugged the ball. My swing short, func-
tional and nothing to write home about, the right-hand
barrel of a bank raider's twelve-bore having upset my shoulder turn for all time. Still, I outdrove Bannerman by a
good twenty yards, no great feat since he was giving me
something over forty years. Nobody laughed, but I noticed
nobody applauded either. Still, we were off.

'You use these things?'

Bannerman must have noticed me fiddling with the
switch on my trolley with dire results. I said, 'I'm afraid
not. You'd better show me.'

He showed me, easy when you know how. A simple twist
grip affair not unlike the throttle of a motorcycle with an
override that enabled one to lock the thing on at a chosen
speed. Tamed, my trolley whined contentedly ahead of me.

Presumably the thing wouldn't go up hills but on the flat it earned its keep.

'You played here before?' Bob Bannerman asked. Without waiting for an answer he played an eight iron to the green with a nonchalant flip of the wrists, seeming in no way surprised that the ball ended up no more than a yard from the pin.

I said no, I hadn't, doing my best to take his shot as a matter of course. But then if you practise something hour after hour, day after day most of your working life, the trick will never entirely leave you. I took a nine iron and concentrated hard, but even so I only just made the edge of the green. My putt was close but it wasn't in. I was going to concede Bannerman's yard but by the time I'd got my mouth open he'd holed out one-handed anyway.

'Tell me about Segal,' I said. 'Isn't he supposed to have beaten you in some kind of service championship during the war?'

'Aye. A nice enough man. But I wasn't knowing him terribly well, you'll understand.' Well, no. Our clever little carts whirred up the ride ahead of us to the second tee. One hundred and eighty-five yards. Par 3.

'I suppose not.'

'Of course he wore well. Americans do, as a rule. They look after themselves with diets and that kind of thing.'

I looked at Bob Bannerman as he selected a five iron, still lean and fit and his own man. I doubted if he weighed a pound more than he had the last time we'd played and he'd certainly never dieted.

I said, 'Tell me about the time he beat you.'

'Oh aye.' Old Bob found the green without difficulty and waited politely until I'd done the same. As we walked after our balls he said, 'To tell the truth, laddie, it was one hell of a long time ago. It were getting towards the end of the war, and someone thought it would be a good idea to have a few sporting fixtures between our lads and the Yanks. Of course it wasn't that easy, seeing as how we played different games. But golf were the same, so they fixed up a tournament. A right shambles it was, too. All right for someone like me, because sport was my job, but half the lads were sandwiching games in between their ordinary flying duties. They held the last rounds here, at Steeple Thurston. That was when young Segal beat me.'

'Making a double eagle—an albatross.'

'Aye.' We reached the green and both two-putted. Bannerman looked at me seriously. 'Look, he played damned well. Oh, I know any hole you play three under par has to be pretty lucky, but he'd been matching me shot for shot all day, and I was Open champion at the time. I was always surprised he didn't do more later.'

'I think he wanted to make money,' I said. 'And forty years ago golf wasn't as profitable as it is these days.'

Bannerman smiled wistfully, remembering days when a hundred pounds was big money. 'You're right, laddie, as I know to my cost.'

We had a pretty good round. The fact that I was hitting further and was something like half his age puts an edge on even equal handicaps, and by the seventeenth I was actually a hole ahead. It was a fearsomely long hole and I remembered Al Segal's description of it. To Bannerman I said, 'Isn't this the hole he did it? The albatross?'

'Aye. Come to think of it, it was.' He looked out down the fairway, which seemed to go on for ever and narrow with it. There were trees both sides, a tangled mass of willows and whatever the stunted variety is that fenmen use to bind their soil together. What one was left to drive down looked more like a woodland path than a purpose built fairway, and even then it wasn't straight, with a bend from right to left.

I said, 'Not much use playing long and straight here.'

'I remember Segal played a natural fade,' Bannerman told me. 'He chose the right course, all right.'

'Don't you mean he played a draw?' No good comes of correcting one's betters, but a ball that fades swings to the right, which on this hole would have undoubtedly landed it among the trees. So far as I was concerned, Segal would have had to hit a draw to keep on the left inclined fairway.

Bannerman didn't answer, having better things to do, settling up his ball. I noticed that this time he'd chosen his driver, even though he took no more than a half swing, stance closed, the club head whipping through from inside to out. I watched the ball climb steadily in a high arc, swerve slightly left and drop safely on the fairway.

'A draw,' I said. 'Like that.'

Bannerman picked up his tee and put it in his pocket, because tees cost money and everyone knows that stuff doesn't grow on trees. 'No, Mr Straun,' he said patiently. 'I remember it fine. He hit a fade. Captain Segal was left-handed, you'll understand.'

I'd been about to drive myself but changed my mind. 'Was he? Are you sure?'

With something of the testiness of age Bob Bannerman said, 'Of course I'm sure.'

'It was a long time ago.'

'Aye, it was. But you don't forget which way round a man plays.' Bannerman frowned. I'd really upset him. 'Cricket an' tennis players you'd maybe forget. But you'll know for yourself, Mr Straun. Left-handed golf players look downright peculiar.'

He was right, of course. They do. I called up a picture of Albatross Segal getting out of his car and shaking hands. I could see him standing to drive. To putt. No, he'd been the same like everyone else. Well, almost everyone else.

'That's the putter you've taken out of your bag, laddie,' Bannerman was saying.

'You're right,' I said. 'I wasn't concentrating.' I fished out my driver but I still hadn't got my mind on the job because I hooked the ball viciously into the trees on the left. Bannerman didn't even say 'Hard Luck' because he knew as well as I did that it was a rotten drive by any standard.

I said apologetically, 'You were right. Wasn't thinking what I was doing.'

'Aye.'

We trudged after the thing. Rather to my surprise I found it without too much trouble, sitting under some fern. I explored the possibilities of a sand iron but changed my mind and knelt down and hit it, almost parallel with the ground, with a seven iron. It was one of those shots that either works or is a complete disaster, but this time luck was with me and the ball squirted out just enough to reach the mown grass from where I could hit a very reasonable wood not all that far short of the green.

'Grand shot!' Bannerman said.

'Thanks.' I pushed the club back in my bag and started up my electric box of tricks. Half a dozen steps later I stopped dead. 'Blast!'

'What is it, laddie?'

I said, 'That sand iron I tried first, back in the trees. I left it there.' I turned and went back, a great one for losing clubs, which is expensive these days. Bannerman came back with me, only, being organized, he'd switched his trolley off before he left it. Not so, me. By the time I'd located my club and picked it up my wretched vehicle was a hundred yards further on, whining steadily into the bright blue yonder.

Bright something yonder. A blinding flash to the left of the trolley, where the trees met the fairway. The cracking thump of an explosion. Bits of tree, clods of earth tossed high in the sky.

Bob Bannerman said, 'What the hell—'

I said, 'Somebody just killed my trolley.'

CHAPTER 7

'It was a hand grenade.' The kind of statement you lost out on whichever way you play it. Reasonable outrage and you're after cheap drama, casual and dismissive and it's Ealing Studios' British. In the private bar of the *Packet Boat* in the company of Lucy Hayward and Laurie, it sounded even more unlikely than I'd expected.

'You're not saying that some lunatic actually *threw* a hand grenade at you in the middle of a golf course!' Lucy seemed to have lost her customary mildness, which was kind of her. Just the same, I wished she'd up and go. The *Packet Boat* had seemed like a good idea, but we hadn't expected to run into Lucy and the least we could do was ask her to join us.

'Nobody was throwing grenades. How did that get about?' Mine host arrived with our drinks.

Lucy said, 'Thank you, Barney,' thereby jogging my memory. Barney Sutton.

'Proper ol' booby trap, if you ask me. Trip wire to pull the pin out.' Sutton jerked his chin towards me. 'That's right enough, now?'

I said, 'It's likely, at any rate.' Like they always say, word gets around. The girls were looking at me, so I went on, 'A grenade goes up when a sprung lever is allowed to rise. Just gripping the thing in your hand keeps the lever down, but when you throw it, up she comes. A few seconds, then bang! There's a pin with a ring in it that keeps the lever in place while you're carrying it around. Booby-trappers tie the grenade to something solid, hook a wire to the ring and think up ways of tripping people up.'

'And that's what someone was trying to do to you?'

I said, 'I don't know. I just suppose so. Of course I might

have noticed the wire. But when my electric trolley went off on its own it didn't bother to look where it was going and just drove straight into the thing.'

Barney shook his head at my money. 'You have those on the house, boy. Reckon you're due a free drink. The place owes you one.'

'The pub owes me?' I thought I'd misheard him. 'Why?'

'Not the pub, boy. The place. Takes against some folk, they say. Them as not fen born.'

I said, 'Now tell us about the Curse of Wendal.'

Barney shook his head. 'There's no curse of anything. But you like it here or you don't, see? And things go right or they don't. Now tell me fair, do you like being in these parts?'

Well, a fair question. 'No,' I said. 'Not much.'

'That's it, then.' Barney gathered an empty. Glanced over his hunched shoulders. 'But your lady do.' He grinned amiably. 'Now don't you fret, boy.'

Saucy sod. I felt my hackles rise. 'You better ask her.'

Laurie said easily, 'Oh yes, I could get hooked on the big sky—the emptiness. Angus thinks it's a bit creepy, but it's a free country. I honestly can't see it signifies anything.'

'I'm sure you're right,' Lucy said briskly. 'And I'm sure whoever tried to blow Angus up didn't give a damn whether he liked the local scenery or not.' She turned to me. 'Do you think you'll catch him?'

Him? Her? 'Well, I won't,' I said. 'I'm just passing through. I'm leaving this one to you local officer. So far as I'm concerned, I'm just a member of the public.'

'Good,' Laurie said, unnecessarily, I thought. 'Stay that way.'

We wished our host good health and drank, the local brew unfamiliar but palatable. With my adrenalin supply still in overdrive I was inclined to regard the incident as a kind of schoolboyish lark. Bloody silly conclusion, when someone had just tried to kill me, which just went to show one should never make decisions on a high.

Lucy said, 'But I simply don't understand who'd want to do such a thing.'

'Presumably,' I said, 'someone who doesn't like me.'

'But you've only been here a couple of days.'

I drank some more beer and wondered how Bob Bannerman was getting on. He'd taken the whole thing in his stride but the shock might well have some delayed effect on a man of his age. I looked at Lucy over the top of my glass. 'Can you think of any other reason?'

'Someone didn't like the man you were playing with?'

Laurie shook her head. 'By all accounts, *everyone* likes Bob Bannerman. And anyway, he was playing at his own club. If anyone wanted to hurt him they could have done it years ago.'

I looked at her with respect. All the same, Lucy had a valid point. Who was it had it in for me? I said, 'Well frankly, I don't know. The boys at Lincoln will have to work it out.'

A phone rang somewhere behind the bar and Barney limped off to answer it. When he came back I felt a frisson of unease.

'For you, Mr Straun.'

Logically there was no need to be apprehensive, because who knew where I was?

'Straun.'

Chief Superintendent Gareth Evans at Tiverton Street knew, for one. 'Sorry I am to disturb you. Is it a pleasant leave you're having?' Over the phone he sounded like a Welsh MP baying from the back benches.

I said, 'Sitting in decent privacy, I am. And hoping to remain so.'

'Don't mock your betters, man. What are you doing in a common hostelry?' He was slow to take offence.

I said shortly, 'I'm having a drink, damn it. How did you know I was here?'

'An Inspector Higham at Lincoln passed the word you were at Wendal, so I got on to the nick at Easterham. The sergeant there told me where you were staying. No reply from the number he gave me, so—'

'When in doubt try the pub.' It wasn't original, but practical enough. And it didn't answer the obvious question. 'You still haven't said why you wanted me. Or why Higham wanted you, come to that.'

'The other way round, man. I wanted Higham.' Evans's voice sounded aggrieved. 'The Foreign Office breathing down my neck, look you.'

'Oh God!' I said. 'Not Todhunter.' Adrian Todhunter haunted my waking thoughts like a mediæval curse, forever making outrageous demands in the name of international friendship and cooperation. Occasionally—very occasionally—he had tried bludgeoning me into agreeing direct. Most times he played safe and got my masters to see things his way. Like now? I said, 'All right, break it to me. What does that bastard want this time?'

The voice in my handset crackled, quavered and finally decided that it would go along with the question. 'He'd heard about Steegle—Spiegal?—'

'Segal,' I prompted him.

'He'd heard that Segal had been killed. A prominent sporting figure is what he called him. Worried, he was, about repercussions if anything was hushed up.'

I mastered an urge to beat the handset to pieces against the wall. There are no arms, no armour against fate. Gareth Evans would have got back to me if he'd had to beam himself by satellite. Barely raising my voice, I said, 'What does he mean by hushed up? The man was killed accidentally.'

'Coroner's verdict?'

'There hasn't been an inquest yet. But there's absolutely nothing to suggest that it was anything else.'

'And the man that was drowned last night?'

How in hell had Gareth Evans heard about Whitton? Through Devenish, I supposed, although that presupposed there was now a direct communication link established. Well, fine. It was nothing to do with me. Aloud I said, 'The man's name was Whitton and he was drowned while fooling around in a fen in the middle of the night. The incidents could hardly be connected in any way. It's certainly got nothing to do with Todhunter.'

There was a pause. Had Gareth Evans smoked, one would have said he was lighting a cigarette, but he didn't smoke. What he was doing was drawing a kind of child's house on his notepad. A door in the middle and windows each side. During a long and tricky telephone conversation I'd watched him construct very complex habitations indeed.

Finally: 'It seems someone informed the American Embassy about Segal. Well known man he was, see?'

I couldn't imagine Higham taking it on himself to do that but maybe someone had given him the nod. But even so—

I said, 'The American Embassy must be aware that Segal was a pretty ordinary real estate agent from somewhere in Ohio. International weighting, zero. What's more, shooting accidents are fairly common. I'm told that over there it's happening all the time.'

'A golfer called Joseph Getz was shot and killed while playing in Texas earlier this year. He was a big wheel in the CIA. They've persuaded Todhunter that there may be a connection.'

I felt sanity slipping from me. Suppressing an urge to scream, I forced my memory to reluctantly regurgitate something I had read about Joseph Getz. I said, 'His wife shot him with a hunting rifle because he was playing around with her sister. It had *nothing* to do with Albatross Segal. Nor his job, even if he was CIA.'

'Well, spend a couple of days up there and make some kind of a report. Just so that Todhunter's got something to show.' Gareth Evans added magnanimously, 'We'll make the time up to you.'

I said, 'The local force will shoot me on sight if I start making inquiries up here.'

'No they won't,' said the voice in the telephone. 'That's been taken care of.'

I should have remembered those words, because they were always cropping up when Adrian Todhunter of the Foreign Office was around. I put the phone down and went to join the ladies. People were saying it all the time. 'Why does this have to happen to me?' I said it this time but I didn't get an answer either.

I felt it again, the curious hostility of the landscape, as we walked back to the farm, and I wondered if anyone else noticed it. Apart from Barney Sutton, that harbinger of doom. Maybe the place had liked it better when it was at the bottom of the sea, which was an engagingly fanciful idea but not really a runner. Most of Holland had been at sea at one time or another and I didn't get the creeps there.

I said, 'We should have got out of this bloody place the first day. Got a tow or something.'

'Well, another couple of days won't kill us.' Laurie was doing her best to cheer me up but I was reluctant; moreover, we'd left Lucy Hayward to her shopping, so there was no longer any need for me to do the social bit.

I said, 'If you believe it'll be only two days you'll believe anything.'

'Do you still think Segal's death was accidental?'

'I still can't see how it could be anything else.' But that

was dodging the issue and I knew it. I said, 'Bob Bannerman swears Segal was left-handed.'

'And was he?'

'Not when he played with me, he wasn't. Played like anyone else.'

She looked at me doubtfully. Laurie's eyes were much the same size as other people's but the huge glasses she wore were for real and the lens magnification made them look enormous. 'He could be a shifted sinistral.'

I said, 'Shifted sinistrals are naturally left-handed people who've been brought up right-handed. Whatever you are in your twenties, you stay.'

'Maybe Bob Bannerman remembered wrong.'

Well yes, maybe. But I didn't think it likely. I thought gloomily of the grenade at Steeple Thurston. At least there was something wholesomely definite about that. Someone had tried to booby-trap me, an unfriendly act that I couldn't begin to explain. I said, 'Day one, Albatross Segal gets killed. Day two, Whitton is drowned. Day three, someone tries to blow me up. Can you see any connection?'

'No.'

I said, 'Neither can I. But there's either a connection or life's extraordinarily hazardous in these parts . . .'

We walked on in silence for a bit before I added, 'If I can hire a car somewhere I think I'll go into Cambridge tomorrow and do a little historical research. Want to come?'

Laurie frowned. 'Darling, I promised Lucy I'd go into Peterborough with her. Would you mind?'

'No,' I said. 'Of course not.' I hadn't really expected her to come, and I wondered why.

She asked, 'How long will this research take?'

'Probably longer than I expect,' I told her. 'It always does.'

'Well, stay the night if you get held up. Better than driving in the dark when you're dog tired.'

'All right.'

There wasn't a wide selection of cars for hire in the immediate vicinity of Wendal Fen but a few phone calls got me a down-at-heel Ford Escort and a warning of dire penalties if I didn't bring it back whole. Cambridge was seventy miles over flat and mostly empty roads, and I made the city in two hours, which was just as well because the narrow streets were crammed with what I soon learned was an ever-present traffic snarl-up. Bicycles filled up what few spaces there were between cars and I blessed the happy chance that had led me to dumping the Escort on the outer fringe. The Tourist Information Centre wasn't difficult to find and an amiable girl peered up at me from between a wall of leaflets and told me where I'd find the Allied Air Veterans' Association.

'14 St Michael's,' she told me without hesitation. 'Second floor. Is it RAF or USAAF?'

'USAAF.' I gave mental thanks to the Real Estaters Golf Society, an organization that got its facts right. I suppose by appearances I should have been RAF but she didn't look surprised.

'Ask for Miss Lorimer.'

'Lorimer?'

'That's right. Lois Lorimer. She's got the details of all the wartime American airfields.' She paused, this helpful girl. 'It *is* an American airfield you're interested in?'

I said, 'Well, yes. An American pilot, as a matter of fact.'

'Lois will help you. She's a super girl.'

The spectral touch on the shoulder. There could, of course, be two Lois Lorimers but I knew there weren't.

My Lois had been a long-legged travel courier from Baltimore whose charges had been caught carrying considerable quantities of proscribed drugs into Britain. Unknowingly, as it turned out, but it had kept me busy for a week. Quite a week, one way or another, but only a week, because there was Angie and Sam and someone back in Baltimore called Fred. End of story. Not a dry eye in the house.

I thanked the girl at the Information desk, that bearer of glad tidings, and headed in the direction of St Michael's, square B2 on the city map and walkable in ten minutes. She was standing looking at a notice pinned to the wall when I went through the door, and she looked round.

I said, 'Hello, Lois.'

I can't remember that she said anything. I do know that once, years before, I'd thought I'd seen her again walking down Jermyn Street and the discovery that it was really a stranger had done nothing to lessen the initial jolt. I'd learned a lot, somewhat later than was good for me, from Lois, and I had no desire to learn it all over again.

She looked at me for what seemed a long time but was probably only a second or two. Then she said, 'Well, hi!' and came over to the counter, near enough for me to catch her perfume. I didn't notice what she was wearing, only that her face hadn't changed, nor her voice, nor the way she moved. I don't suppose that even as a young girl Lois had ever been conventionally pretty because her features were too big or irregular or something, shortcomings she must have made up for in some secret way because I had never managed to look at anyone else when she was in the room. A woman can be remarkably like a round of golf, of consuming interest to the man concerned but a bore in the telling. Sufficient to say that for me, once and too briefly, Lois had been my girl, *the* girl, and it didn't need what my old great-aunt had bequeathed me of the Sight to know that, investigations notwithstanding, lightning can and does strike twice. I knew the score. As of now I was pushing my luck.

Six—seven years. What does one say? What I did say was, 'I didn't expect to find you here.' True, too. I hadn't even known she was in the country, let alone Cambridge.

'Are you still a policeman?' She was not a fidgety woman. She just stood there, totally at her ease. More than could be said of me.

'I'm afraid so.' It had been with Lois that I'd discovered, thinking myself alone in that knowledge, that a man and a woman can know to a moment when they become lovers. A look, a touch, and the courtship over, the contract sealed. The act itself may have to wait on time and place but that it will happen is agreed. It had been that way with us, all those years ago. I heard myself saying, 'That's why I'm here.'

She had a surprisingly deep laugh, sceptical, uninhibited, entirely joyous.

'Damn it,' I said, 'I didn't know you had this job.'

'My dear, I believe you. Tell me why you're here.' Her rather clipped, Ivy League American was marginally softer than I remembered it.

I said, 'I'm trying to find out something about an American officer who flew here during the war.' She didn't say anything so I went on, 'Someone told me your organization fixes itineraries for USAAF veterans, and I thought you might have at least some official records to work from.'

'Well, yes. Units. Aircraft. Stations—things like that. Not people.' She waggled her long, slender hands dismissively, and I saw she was wearing a wedding ring. Current marriage? Old marriage? Lorimer was her maiden name, but that meant nothing. Lots of married women worked under their original name. She was saying, 'I mean, we *got* the people. They come to us. It's the places they want to know about.'

I said, 'You mean they don't remember where they were stationed?'

She smiled. 'Sure they do. But so many of the old airfields just aren't there any more. Most of them have had corn growing instead of runways for more than forty years and the sites take some locating. When the vets want to go round a working farm they like us to fix permission, and of course hotels. Mostly they come in groups, so we lay on minibus transport and so on. There's a lot to it.'

'Quite an industry.'

'It's kind of rewarding. Most of them are sort of stepping back in time—I think they feel, given the chance, they could still fly a B-24 to Berlin and back. And we still get widows. You know that? Still get ladies wanting to see the places some poor dead guy knew back before I was born.'

I said, 'My chap flew from Wendal Fen. Eighth Tactical Air Force. B-24s.'

Lois frowned. 'Lincolnshire? 9th TAF, surely?'

'I'm told it was 8th.'

She went into a hutch-like office and prodded keys in front of a computer screen. After a while she said over her shoulder, 'You're right. Most of the 8th was in Norfolk but it looks as though a few bits crept up. 901, 907, 909 and 932 Squadrons were stationed at Wendal from 1943 on. B-24s.' She paused. 'Want to know about the airfield?'

I said, 'I'll take anything you've got.'

'It wasn't built until 1942. The land was leased off someone called Hayward, the contractors were Matherson and Son of Peterborough. Land surrendered May 1946. Most of it's gone back to farm but the main runway's still there and most of the perimeter track. I'll have a map on file and probably the odd photograph. Wendal doesn't get many visitors—like I said, most of the Eighth Air Force vets head for Norfolk. You want to make a note of all this?'

I laid my Philips micro-recorder down in front of me. 'I taped it. Is that all right?'

'Sure. Why not?'

'Can you see if you've got anything on crews? Anything at all?'

Lois frowned. 'Like I said, we don't get asked a lot about

crew. But there's a terrific Second Air Division memorial library in Norwich—you could try there. Right here, we've got most of the books written about local airfields—some of them are incredible research jobs. And we've got books of old press cuttings. But it'll take time to look.'

'Give me the stuff. I'll look.'

'Like hell you will.' She gave me the wary, hands-off look that I remembered from way back. 'Come back at five. We close then. If I've got anything, you can have it.'

I went off and kicked my heels. Cambridge is as good a place as any for killing a few hours. I did the Fitzwilliam Museum, toured the Backs, ate an unhurried lunch at an ancient inn, bought some books. There had been a moment in the first few days of our knowing each other when I'd handed Lois a book I'd just bought and our fingers had touched and our eyes had met and I think we had both known in that moment that something out of the ordinary lay in wait for the two of us. In the end, it never did happen, no fault of ours.

She was waiting at the entrance to No. 14 when I got there, a little before five, holding a briefcase like any one of the faculty. Lois said, 'I locked up early. Shall we walk along the Backs?'

We joined the straggling groups of undergraduates on a bridge across the Cam. By now the trees were casting deep shadows on the stretch of grass flanking the towpath and the first leaves of autumn crunched underfoot. A punt slid silently by. I watched the boy recovering the wet pole with casual grace, leaving a trail of droplets on the sleek surface of the river behind him. Lois dropped on to the grass, her back against a tree, and I sat down beside her. Odd that she, an American, was more at home here than I.

Lois started to open her case. 'You can relax. I got the press cuttings.' Her left hand was stretched flat on the grass beside me and I reached out and touched her wedding ring.

She didn't look at me. 'Look, I got your goddam cuttings! Isn't that enough?'

'No,' I said. I wished I was a simple policeman again but it's no easy business being a crafty amalgam of what one is and what one wants to be at the right time. 'No, it isn't enough.'

She took her hand away and sorted out the papers she'd brought. 'We didn't arrange this, it just happened. But now that it *has* happened—'

'Yes?'

'Suppose you don't ask anything about me, and I don't ask about you. We're just here for the day. How about that?'

I said, 'Agreed.' Could one really suspend one's life for twenty-four hours? I didn't know, but one could try.

She twisted round and looked at me. 'Darling, you're not exactly expansive. You could ask a girl to dinner, for a start.' She passed me a couple of newspaper cuttings. 'Any use?'

I looked at the first, a yellowed clip from some local paper, dated 3rd August 1944. It showed a bare-headed young man grinning and holding up a silver trophy. The headline read:

OPEN CHAMPION BEATEN BY SHOT
IN A MILLION
USAAF Pilot's Feat

and the caption filled in the rest of the story.

Golfing history was made today at Steeple Thurston Golf Club, which staged the final of the All England Inter-Services Golf Trophy. Captain J. Bazil of 901 Bomber Squadron USAAF took time out from bombing Hitler's Germany to defeat Staff Sergeant Robert Bannerman,

RAF. Sgt Bannerman is, of course, better known as Bob
Bannerman, the reigning British Open Champion. After
a close last round, Captain Bazil pulled off a surprise win
by holing his second shot on the Par 5 seventeenth hole
for an unprecedented Albatross. Bazil said, 'It sure was
the shot of a lifetime.'

The second cutting was from something called the *Wendal
Warrior*, presumably the squadron newsheet, which carried
much the same text but didn't run to a picture.

I folded up Lois's newspaper cuttings and gave them
back to her. 'Will you have dinner with me?'

'Yes, please.'

It seemed unlikely that even in wartime a golf tournament would have had two winners. But if James A. Bazil
had beaten Bob Bannerman all those years ago, where did
Albatross Segal come in?

What with one thing and another, it was getting to be
quite a day.

CHAPTER 8

Home to Wendal Fen by way of Steeple Thurston. It had rained during the night and left the sky with the kind of pale washed light that persuades people to try their hand at watercolour. Villages of Dutch gabled houses and curiously anglicized Dutch names, with here and there a still complete windmill poking up against the horizon. An odd bit of country, to which the water men from Holland had come briefly but left a significant part of themselves behind.

It was midday by the time I reached the golf club, fairly busy judging by the number of cars in the car park. Most of the members must have still been out on the course because the bar was almost empty. I asked the steward if Bob Bannerman was about.

'No, sir. Haven't seen Mr Bannerman at all this morning. Probably caught up with his garden.'

I hadn't known, but could imagine old Bob fiddling around with roses. I said, 'I wanted to have a word with him. I suppose he lives near here?'

'Myrtle Cottage. It's the last place on the left before you come to the Pedley crossroads. A couple of miles at the most.'

I thanked him and headed the Escort that way, eye cocked for ye olde cottage with roses round the door and a myrtle tree in the garden, always supposing that myrtle *was* a tree. Fortunately there was a name board on the gate of the large modern bungalow that turned out to be the last building before the crossroads. But true enough there was a sizeable and immaculate garden wherein a happily scruffy Bob Bannerman snipped fussily at his roses.

'Angus, laddie!' The lines on his face were no more than

comfortable wrinkles, his movements brisk. Most sports take their toll in the end, when the muscle goes and everything sags. Hopefully, not golf. Certainly it had been a good friend to Bob, eighty-plus and playing to his age without giving it a thought. He said, 'Now, do you know anything about roses?'

'Not a thing.'

'Then you'll be having a dram.'

'I'll be having a beer,' I said. A couple of Scots drams and I'd be ripe for the breathalyzer and the front pages. *Another police officer found drunk at the wheel.*

'Och, if ye must make these silly laws, I suppose you'd better obey them.'

I said, 'Police don't make laws, they just enforce them. It's Parliament who make silly laws. It's their full-time job.'

We went indoors. Everything bright, spick and span and still with the touch of a woman. I wondered how long since Bob's wife had died. There was a glass case with God knows how many golfing pots, and a small one on its own that houses the miniature claret jug that's given to every Open champion.

Bob fetched the drinks and his pale blue eyes gave me a going-over. 'I thought policemen never drank on duty.'

I swallowed some beer, that still unfamiliar local brew. 'Who says I'm on duty?'

'I do, laddie, for one.'

'All right,' I said. 'Tell me what you remember about Al Segal.'

'Och, I remember the albatross fine.' Bannerman looked reminiscent. 'It was no laughing matter at the time, but it's the kind of lucky shot that happens now an' then, like a hole in one. In fact it's *better* than that. On a short hole you can see the green, but I remember well that he made his second shot blind. But it still went in.'

'A fluke,' I said.

Bannerman nodded. 'Aye, you could call it that. For an amateur it was a fluke—the man would never do it again if he tried for a hundred years.'

And not just for an amateur, I thought. I remembered hearing about a magazine who challenged a top pro to get a hole in one. He'd tried all day, dumping literally hundreds of balls on to the green of a short par 3 hole. Apparently the green had looked as if there'd been a hailstorm, but he'd never got a single ball into the hole.

I said, 'Apart from shooting that albatross, what do you remember about the man himself?'

Bannerman frowned. 'Och, it's forty years an' a thousand games ago. I remember he was a nice enough young fellow.'

'When you met him again the other day, Segal asked if you remembered him and you said yes.' I had some more beer just to let the question sink in. 'Well—did you?'

Old Bob studied his pre-lunch dram, not a man to look guilty but today something not far off. He said apologetically, 'You know well, Straun, that people like fine to be remembered. They don't ask themselves is it likely that I'd know the face of a man just because I played a round with him nigh on half a century ago. You ask me if I recognized Mr Segal. Well, the answer's no. I didn't remember the man from Adam.' He looked up from his drink. 'Was that what you wanted to know?'

'It's what I thought you might say.'

We sat there contemplating our drinks. The Scots are not a chatty race, better with outlanders than with each other. Finally Bob Bannerman got round to saying what must have been at the back of his mind all along. 'To tell the truth, I was surprised to see him. But you know the way of it, you think your memory's at fault. Lord knows it is, a good deal of the time.'

'Why were you surprised to see Segal?' I prompted.

'Because it was stuck in my mind the man was dead.

There was talk he'd been killed just a wee while after we'd had our game. An' that he'd left a wife an' bairn into the bargain.'

CHAPTER 9

The Maserati was standing outside the barn when I got back, a sight that would have cheered me considerably twenty-four hours earlier, as transport to another planet. Now it was simply tantalizing, the means by which to go for someone ordered to stay.

I parked the Escort and got behind the wheel of my own car. Whoever had fixed it had done his job well, the gear lever slipped through the selectors smoothly and accurately. Good as new, or better. What was the phrase? To aircraft standards. I got out and a small gust of wind caught at my legs, curiously chill. I glanced up at the few clouds but they were still as a painted backdrop, no wind up there. From an open window I could hear women laughing. Laurie and Lucy. I went in and joined them in the kitchen, the working man's return.

'I must go,' Lucy said after we had made our hellos. She was in jeans and the kind of check shirt lumberjacks are supposed to wear, laughter was kind to her, recapturing the kind of beauty she must have had as a young girl. 'Angus, you've no idea how nice it is to have a woman next door. You don't mind if I call you Angus?'

I said, 'Of course not. But stay where you are.'

'No, I must fly. A major shop in Peterborough—I load up for the week.' She flew.

'I thought the two of you were going shopping yesterday.' The aggressive male, jumping into trouble, as ever, with both feet.

'Lucy couldn't make it yesterday, so I went with Patrick instead.' Laurie was no woman for shooting a sitting duck with just one barrel, she let him have both of them. Bang!

She didn't look defiant or guilty or really anything that I could detect, and God knows I was trying to detect something. Jealousy is a weakness that defies logic, a humiliating weakness come to that, but no easy thing to banish.

I said, 'I suppose Patrick has a weekly raid on the supermarket, too.'

Laurie began to fold up the newspaper she and Lucy had been laughing over. Normally she was not a folder of newspapers but she was this morning. 'He didn't say. When we got there he went off and did his thing, I did mine.' She put the flattened newspaper down and deigned to look up at me. 'He wasn't loaded down with carrier bags when we met up later. Should I have asked him?'

'No. Sorry. Forget it.'

'Darling, are you *jealous* of Patrick?'

I said, 'You know bloody well I am.'

'Idiot.' Then, 'Sorry. I knew it would get you riled. I'm a silly bitch sometimes, and I don't know what got into me.' Then: 'Tell me how you got on.' The cheerful admittance of folly that it would be boorish to reject. Thin ice, though. Too thin for comfort.

I said, 'The chap who beat Bob Bannerman back in 1944 was called Bazil. He was lost over Germany a week or so later, leaving a widow and a child. The character who got himself shot the other day was called Segal. He was a fraud. He never shot an albatross against Bob Bannerman, chances are he never met him.'

Laurie blinked. 'They were two different men?'

I nodded. 'Now supposing—just supposing—that Segal's death wasn't an accident. Suppose someone shot him.'

'So?'

'Suppose I'm not the only one who's confused about this. Wouldn't it be possible for someone to shoot Segal by mistake, thinking he was someone else?'

'Nobody's going to try to kill Bazil if the man's been dead forty years,' Laurie pointed out. 'Besides, your nice Mr Segal sounded genuine enough to me. He knew the place, didn't he? You said yourself that he drove you around.'

I said, 'He could have studied a plan of the airfield somewhere.' But I knew he hadn't. Someone who'd mugged up a load of facts would have tried to impress me with this knowledge and the Albatross had been caught out more than once, seeking buildings long fallen to the bulldozer. Besides which there'd been that indefinable something that told me he was genuine. Albatross Segal may or may not have played that match with Bob Bannerman but I was prepared to swear he'd known Wendal Fen airfield. I stared out across the fields and picked up the rooftops of the village. 'Come on,' I said, 'I'll buy you lunch.'

For a moment I thought she was going to refuse but apparently we were in a state of truce because she asked, 'Charlie's Plaice?'

'No.' I told her. 'Money's no object. We'll try the pub.'

Laurie stood up and pulled her skirt straight. 'And you can ask around and see if anyone remembers what happened to Bazil's widow.'

She didn't miss a trick.

Lunch at the *Packet Boat* was much as one would expect but there are worse things than toasted bacon sandwiches and beer. We sat in the window and did our best not to rub each other up the wrong way. I know I wondered what it was that had gone wrong between us and possibly Laurie felt the same. God knows, we weren't a pair given to emotional traumas, but it was quite a relief when Barney Sutton came clumping on his gammy leg from behind the bar to take our plates away and I could ask him if he'd heard of a widow called Bazil.

'No, boy, can't say as I have.' Singsong Lincolnshire sounding comfortingly regretful. Mine host's lined face and rather dog-like eyes brought to mind an amiable but dim hound. 'If it were wartime, like, I hadn't moved here then.'

'Anyone in the bar who might help?' It was a long shot in any case, because a wartime widow would almost certainly have remarried by now.

Barney shook his head. 'Syd High must be about the eldest an' he's not much over fifty. Be in his pram then.'

Well, yes. I said, 'Can you think of anyone who does go back that far?'

Barney frowned. One of the world's obligers, I could imagine it hurt him to turn down a plea for help. He said reluctantly, 'There are some old chaps around, right enough. But it'll be a waste of time asking.'

Well, he had a point there. It wouldn't have been the young men who'd have known about who'd been married to who in 1944. The chances were most of them had been serving overseas themselves at the time anyway. 'You're right,' I said. 'We want some grey-haired old lady who used to whoop it up at the base when she was a girl. Any suggestions?'

Barney looked doubtful. 'Who's doin' the asking? You or me?'

Laurie smiled faintly. She said, 'He's thinking that your grey-haired old lady will probably have been married to some local lad for the best part of forty years. Maybe she does remember the high old times she used to have with the Yanks but she's not going to let her husband hear about them.'

I looked at Barney hopefully. 'Widows? Elderly spinsters?'

'Dunno, boy. Have to ask around, won't I?'

I said that would be fine but I knew instinctively that he wasn't going to and I didn't altogether blame him. Asking personal questions on one's own account can be sufficiently embarrassing, without taking the job on for other people, and in any case publicans make a point of not getting involved in that sort of thing. But a bell had rung, faint but clear. I waited until the landlord had taken our plates away before I turned to Laurie. 'How about getting your hair washed?'

She looked at me coldly. 'If you want me to chat someone up, what's wrong with the post office?'

I said, 'You'll need more time. I want you to find out where Darren Penney's grandmother lives.'

'You mean the boy who—'

'Yes,' I said. 'That one. If I'm not mistaken he's not just dark-haired, he's part coloured. Perhaps a quarter. What in the old slave days they used to call a quadroon.'

Laurie frowned. 'Does it matter?'

'For God's sake,' I said, 'socially it doesn't matter a damn. In the context of what I'm still here for it could matter a lot. If Darren's a quarter coloured, one of his parents was half coloured. Which means one pair of his grandparents was one black and one white. I can't very well ask him because the boy's made himself scarce. But if he's seventeen, it means his parents could well have been born about the end of the war, which leads us to the reasonable supposition that his grandmother married a black American serviceman.'

'What makes you think she's still alive?' When so inclined, Laurie could be extraordinarily unsupportive. 'And even if she is, she may not want to talk about it. Lots of girls had babies during the war without being married. Would *you* want to talk about a little accident you had half a century ago?'

I said, 'The day Darren played at being Billy the Kid someone said something about his grandmother. So he's *got* a grandmother and I'd like to talk to her.' I wished Laurie was a WPC or, better still, Sergeant Endicott, because I'm not good at the explaining bit, which tends to waste time.

Like the centurion in the Bible, I say unto this man come
and he cometh and to that man go and he goeth, the only
way to run a shop. I hoped Laurie wasn't expecting me to
explain why it was her job to make the inquiries because I
was getting edgy and I had no wish to make things more
difficult between us than they were already.

Laurie was looking at Doreen's. There was a light on
inside but no sign to suggest that the local wenches spent
their lunch hour getting their hair fixed. She said, 'I'll be
as quick as I can.'

We looked at each other with mutual regard. Maybe
there was something in telepathy after all.

Somewhere between the rinse and blowdry it turned out
that Darren's grandmother had moved from Wendal and
now lived in ever such a nice bungalow at Stoke Cross.
Stoke Cross, according to the signpost, was five miles out
on the Lincoln road. Ungratefully, I left Laurie at the barn
and went visiting on my own.

'I wasn't expecting you, but do come in.' Her name was
Mrs Marion Penney, late sixties, putting on weight a bit
but still a sort of faded prettiness that lasts with some
women more than one might expect. Like she said, she
wasn't expecting me, but the flowered cotton dress was
cheap but cheerful.

'I was just having my tea. Would you like a cup?'

I said that a cup would be nice and she sat me down and
fetched a cup and saucer. The bungalow was modern and
well maintained, the room more comfortable than I'd
expected. What *had* I expected? Less, I supposed. I took in
the fitted carpet, the three-piece suite, the television with a
video beneath it, a central heating radiator against a freshly
papered wall. Solidly comfortable. Mr Penney, whoever
he'd been, must have left her with a bob or two. Well, why
not? I recalled a few chatelaines of honoured name whose

grandsons were deader beat than Darren by a long chalk.

'You'll be wanting to talk about Darren, then?' Mrs Penney handed me my tea.

'I'd rather talk about his grandfather.'

'Oh.' She gave me a look that was more disappointment than resentment. A small sigh. 'Now what would you want to do that for? Such a long time ago he was.'

'I know, Mrs Penney.' The daily round, the sordid task. Sometimes I was less than in love with my job. I said, 'I put that rather badly. I really only want to know if he was an American serviceman.'

It wasn't the kind of question I'd have got away with in London, where I'd have been told quick enough to mind my own bloody business. In the sticks people were too civilized to do that and I, of course, took advantage of the fact.

'Yes, he was on the base. A sergeant. The Americans call them sergeants, though they wore their stripes upside down.'

'They still do,' I said.

'Do they now!' Mrs Penney smiled unexpectedly so that I got a fleeting glimpse of what had hooked an upside down sergeant in the middle of a war. She said, almost as though with surprise, 'Eh, he was a lovely man, Elijah. That funny. Always making a girl laugh.' Worse ways of being remembered.

I said gently, 'What happened to him, Mrs Penney?'

'He ran into something in his jeep. At night it was. I suppose it had been raining or something.' Perhaps she'd known once but like she said, it had been a long time ago. 'Going to get married we were. Not just because there was a baby coming, he said. Just because we got on, like. But what with one thing and another we left it too late.'

I said, 'That sort of thing must have happened quite a bit during the war.'

'Of course it did, dear. People understood.' She looked away, contemplating her own times, when life really had been real and earnest and girls had babies because they were in love and not because they wanted a free house at the taxpayer's expense. Mrs Penney fiddled with her handkerchief. 'In the end it was Harry who didn't understand.'

'Harry?'

'My boy. I called him after my Dad. But he blamed Elijah, you see.' I thought she was going to say because he was coloured but if 1940s Lincolnshire had its prejudices, that wasn't one of them, because Mrs Penney said almost primly, 'He couldn't forgive Elijah for not marrying me.'

More likely he couldn't forgive his father for making him a bastard, I thought, but in the long run it probably came to the same thing. My eye had caught a silver-framed photograph of what was pretty obviously a young Mrs Penney, flanked by two young children. One dark, presumably young Harry, the other a fair, pretty girl. Who she?

I said, 'And Mr Penney?'

'Geoff and I were married in 1955. He passed on five years ago. Heart.'

'And how did Harry get on with his stepfather?'

Mrs Penney visibly relaxed. 'Oh, ever so well. I think Harry would have liked Geoff for his dad, really. Right from the start he said he was going to call himself Harry Penney.'

I said, 'I suppose lots of your friends married Americans from the base.'

'Some.'

'Anyone who married a Captain Bazil?'

Mrs Penney looked at me. She could have looked startled or confused or just plain fed up but she didn't. She just looked at me and her blue eyes were as steady as rocks. 'No, dear. I didn't know anyone called that.'

'You're sure?'

She answered with a touch of spirit, 'Well, of course I'm sure. I mean, Elijah was a sergeant. I didn't have much to do with officers.'

'No,' I said, 'I suppose not.' I let my eyes go past her to the picture on the bookshelf. 'That's Harry with you over there, isn't it?'

She followed the direction of my eyes. 'Well—yes. He must have been about four then.'

'And the girl?' I'd thought for a moment that she might be Penney's daughter but the child was too old.

Mrs Penney's face took on a stubborn look. 'Just a friend. A friend of Harry's. They used to play together.'

'Where's Harry now?' I hoped to God he was all right, because Mollie Penney didn't seem to have too much luck with her men.

'He works on an oil rig,' Mrs Penney said. 'It's good money, of course, but he's away a lot.' She hesitated, reluctant to confide in a stranger. 'That's why Darren's so wild, I suppose. Last year his mother went off with a fellow from Leicester. I shouldn't be saying this but I never did like her. Harry could have done so much better but you know how it is.'

I nodded. From personal experience, mercifully, no. But as a policeman I understood all right. I sensed rather than saw the woman relax as I said, 'Yes, I know. You've been very helpful, Mrs Penney, but there's just one more thing . . .'

'Yes, dear?'

'If Elijah hadn't been killed, what would your married name have been?'

Mrs Penney drew herself up in her chair. 'If Elijah and I had been wed,' she said, 'I'd have been Mrs Elijah Pine-coffin.'

Lucy Hayward, née Pinecoffin, wasn't in the house when I got back and the sixteen-year-old village girl who helped with the cleaning had no suggestions as to where she might be. She didn't come up with what used to be called a knowing look but a certain smugness served the same purpose. Precious little happens in the country that the locals don't know about, so very likely Hayward wouldn't have been able to pinch a barmaid's bottom without half the county saying ho! ho!, let alone construct a forty-foot-long funeral boat. On the other hand, there's a rural tolerance for behaviour that would get an urban counterpart classed as barking mad. I went out round the back of the Dutch barns and saw Lucy's car was at the entrance to the old bunker. I might not be exactly welcome but at least she didn't mind people knowing she was there. I went down the steps and pushed open the door.

'How are you with a band saw?' She was looking at me over the top of her drawing-board, a pencil between her teeth, which made her sound like a patient in the dentist's chair. She took it out and straightened her back. 'Saul could do with a hand.'

He was out of sight somewhere in the region of the stern, hidden by the great swell of the boat's hull. I'd forgotten how enormous the thing was. The upward curve of the sternpost towered a dozen feet above my head, climbing out of the great oaken keel. Forty foot long, maybe twelve feet in the beam. No wonder the longboats had drawn no more than three feet. Easy to imagine them slipping silently up the estuaries, the huge sweeps paddling the warriors upstream. A real ship would have had a carving at the top of the sternpost, a dragon's head or something equally appropriate. God, but they must have looked terrifying, looming out of the mist, loaded with thirty or forty savages who used terror as a stock in trade. Loot and pillage, oh my word.

'Who is it?' Saul was calling from wherever he was behind the stern.

'It's Angus, dear.' Odd how some women unconsciously speak to their men as to a child.

'Does he want to help?' I looked at the overlapping planks above me, each lashed to the ribs with the withers of some kind of root. I remembered reading somewhere that the arrangement allowed the planks to flex against the pounding of the sea, but that did little to explain how Saul had managed to reproduce the technique so exactly. One never ceases to be impressed by the profligate skills of the true enthusiast, the nutters who create wonders as they follow some kind of fuzzy personal star.

'I'm a metal man myself,' I said. 'Can't do a thing with wood.'

He didn't answer. I suppose he'd already forgotten I was there. I looked at Lucy's drawing. So far as I could make out she was scaling up a section of a much smaller plan, probably details of some historic vessel. Her draughtsmanship was untrained but clear and workmanlike. I got the impression that it was something she'd taught herself, though it was hard to imagine any woman going to that amount of trouble for the sake of the bee in someone else's bonnet.

'Hēt him ȳŏ-lidan gōdne gegyrwan,' Hayward observed. 'He ordered the building of a stout ship.'

'Look,' I said, 'I want to speak to you.'

Lucy said, 'You are speaking to me.'

'Not here.'

She looked at me speculatively and I thought, not for the

first time, what an amazing looking girl she must have been. What in God's name had persuaded her to marry Hayward? But come to that, by what strange compulsion does anyone marry anyone in a world so full of mismatches?

'All right.' She raised her voice over the sound of the band saw. 'Saul!'

'Yes?'

'I'm just going to the house for a minute. Angus wants something.'

> Fyrst forð gewāt;   flota wæs on ȳðum,
> bāt under beorge.   Beornas gearwe
> on stefn stigon—   strēamas wundon,
> sund wið sande;

Hayward peered at me like some mad schoolmaster. 'Translate!'

His wife caught my eye and shook her head. Even the best of them would get bored with an unremitting diet of Anglo Saxon epic. I said,

> 'Time moved on. The boat lay ready at
> 'the foot of the cliff. The well-armed
> 'warriors climbed up into the prow as
> 'the tide stirred against the sand.'

I added, 'Roughly.'

Hayward grunted. 'Very roughly.'

Lucy put down her pencil and we went out into the twilight and back to the house.

'You'd better come into the office. We shan't be disturbed there.'

The room she took me to was just that, a couple of desks, shelves lined with box files, an Amstrad PC, the odds and ends of business administration. There was a leather chair for visitors, mine, and one for her behind what was presumably her own desk. She crossed her arms in front of her and leaned on them and I got the feeling I was late for an interview. 'Yes, Angus?'

I said, 'Yes, Miss Pinecoffin.'

We regarded each other. Who was it wrote *In Praise of Older Women*? I couldn't remember but whoever it was would have taken to Lucy Pinecoffin or Hayward or whatever. Her beauty hung about her like a fragment of music or a half-remembered verse, not enough for total recall but enough to hint at what you'd missed. Just sitting at her desk in an over-large sweater was enough to raise fashion photographers from their graves reaching for their Hasselblads.

'Lucy Pinecoffin.' She repeated the name as though she hadn't heard it for years. 'Yes, that used to be my name. Does it matter?'

'It depends,' I said. 'Suppose you tell me what you know about Albatross Segal and James Bazil.'

If she was surprised she didn't show it. 'Suppose you tell me what *you* know.'

I sighed. 'Frankly, not a lot. I know that the late Captain Segal, who I played golf with the other day, wasn't the man who beat Bob Bannerman forty-odd years ago. That famous albatross was made by a Captain Bazil who got himself shot down and killed a couple of weeks later, leaving the English girl he'd married a widow with a young child.' I paused, because that was just about all I knew for a fact, and instinct told me not to bluff on about knowing more. I said, 'I know that when Bazil died, Segal stepped into his shoes. Exactly how or why I don't know, but that's something I'll find out. There's a lady in Cambridge who spends her entire working life checking out American aircrew who served in these parts. Give her time and she'll come up with the facts. In the meantime it would speed things up if you'd tell me something yourself.'

Lucy frowned. 'What makes you suppose I can?'

I said, 'The fact that James Bazil was your father and Mrs Penney your foster mother will do for a start.'

She didn't exactly subside into a quivering mass so I assumed she'd guessed what was coming. But she still looked at me with a certain defiance. 'You're guessing.'

'You're dead right I'm guessing,' I told her. 'But I shan't be guessing once I've had someone look up your birth certificate. I don't know whether you took your foster mother's name legally or not but the Public Records Office will have you the way you were born so you may as well tell me the rest.'

She thought that one over and I don't suppose she liked it very much. It's surprising how often people forget the fact that we're all down in black and white in that singularly ugly building just across the river from Strand-on-the-Green and that however dodgy our deaths may be it's very difficult to mess about with our births.

'The swap,' I prompted her. 'When did Segal become a champion golfer?'

'Pretty soon after the match.' Now she'd made up her mind to tell me what she knew Lucy spoke briskly and without hesitation. 'You probably know that USAAF air-crew were posted home once they'd completed twenty-five missions. An awful lot of them were shot down before they got that far, but Segal managed to survive. He must have been relieved, to put it mildly, but there was a snag. For some time he'd been having an affair with a brother officer's wife. Jamie Bazil's wife, Eileen.'

'Did Bazil know?'

Lucy shook her head. 'I'm quite sure he didn't. Of course all I know is what Aunt Marion—Mrs Penney—told me over the years, but she used to say that my father was one of those people who did everything well without even trying.'

I nodded. 'There are people like that.'

'Apparently it drove Frank Segal up the wall. He was

mad about golf and spent hours practising. He was pretty good, but although my father never seemed to work at it he was still better. When he won that tournament it must have been the last straw. Sometimes I think that having an affair with my mother was his way of getting his own back.'

I said, 'Do you know anything about how your father came to get killed?'

'Oh yes.' Lucy looked at me steadily. 'He was killed because of Frank Segal. Frank asked my father if he'd stand in for him on a mission. He claimed he had some vital personal business that had to be attended to. I can guess what it was, because later that day some of the other boys saw Frank and my mother together in a local pub. But by then my father had agreed to take his place on the mission. He never came back.'

I said, 'That couldn't have made Frank over popular.'

'I don't suppose it mattered that much,' Lucy told me. 'He only had another couple of missions to fly and then he was off back home. When he went, he took my mother with him.'

'Leaving you behind?'

'Leaving me behind.'

It sounded horrific but in fact it was pretty small beer compared with some of the things mothers do to their children and maybe nobody is totally sane in the middle of a war. But the mechanics worried me, because I seemed to remember stories of boatloads of GI brides setting off to rejoin their husbands in the early days of peace. I asked, 'How did Segal manage to take your mother with him, just like that?'

Lucy waggled her hands dismissively. 'The American army wasn't *like* ours. There were plenty of B-17s going back to the States in 1944. A USAAF captain who'd done a full tour could get a free ride for just about anybody, let alone his wife, if he had the right friends.'

'*Was* she his wife?'

'Oh my dear, I don't know.' Lucy shook her head. 'I suppose so. She'd been widowed, after all.'

'So Segal had got his friend's wife,' I said. 'What did he do next?'

Lucy laughed. 'When he got back to America? He went to college.'

I'd forgotten Albatross Segal's masterly move to the sports-orientated college of wherever it was. I said, 'I know. He told me about that. I can't understand how he got away with it but he obviously did.'

'I suppose if you pick your time right, like the middle of a war, you can get away with all sorts of things,' Lucy Hayward said.

'There was an account of the match in the station newspaper,' I remembered. 'Segal edited the thing, so he could easily have printed a one-off special edition featuring himself as the winner instead of Bazil. A sports-conscious American college would hardly have checked up on its accuracy, but they'd have jumped at the chance of signing up an ex-bomber pilot who'd defeated the British Open champion.' I was guessing, of course, but it must have been something like that. So I said to Lucy, 'Now tell me how you came to live with Mrs Penney.'

'My mother left me behind when Frank took her to the States.' Lucy made the statement in the matter-of-fact tones of someone who'd had plenty of time to get used to the idea. 'I can see her point. I mean, I was only eighteen months old and being the kind of bitch she was she probably didn't see much point in lugging surplus baggage. So she dumped me like a hot potato and Mrs Penney fostered me.'

'Why Mrs Penney?'

'I suppose because she got paid.' Lucy paused and waggled her hands. She had very long, slender hands and waggling them gave her the kind of vulnerable look of the well-meaning female who finds it all rather beyond her.

'My mother used to take me round to Mrs Penney on evenings when she wanted to go out with her friends. I'd be put to bed and get picked up next day. Until, of course, the day came when my dear mother dumped me and ran. Just never came back.' Lucy smiled wryly. 'Nobody could have blamed Mrs Penney for handing me over to the authorities, who'd have put me into some kind of home, I suppose. But instead she persuaded them to let her act as a foster mother. She got paid, of course, and I imagine the money was welcome. But that was in the beginning. Afterwards I think she kept me because she was fond of me. I certainly was of her. She was a lovely sort of surrogate mum. She'd had a little boy by a black Master Sergeant called Pinecoffin. She called herself Mrs Pinecoffin because she'd have married Elijah if he hadn't been killed in a road accident, so I called myself Lucy Pinecoffin, so as not to be different.'

'And Mr Penney?'

'Oh, he was nice. He's dead now but he was nice.'

'So why did you leave home?'

'Because I turned out beautiful, I suppose.' The kind of statement only a certain kind of woman can make without embarrassment. She went on, 'It was in the David Bailey days, when trendy photographers were a household word, likewise the better known models. I got a job working in a Knightsbridge boutique, then one day Bailey took a shot of me wearing a leather jacket. I was off.'

Well, I wondered where I'd seen her before. I'd been at school at the time but even in those days schoolboys weren't exactly unconscious of the world around them. Lucy had been eminently pin-up material. I said, 'And then?'

'I met Saul and we got married. The 'sixties thing was just about over by then but it wasn't because of that.' For the first time Lucy hesitated. 'He was different, then. Oh, older than me, but pretty sensible. I'd had loads of fun and it had been marvellous having people make a fuss of me and all that sort of thing. One didn't make a lot of money modelling in those days, nothing even approaching what the top girls get today, but I hadn't gone short. Even so, there was a feeling by then that the whole scene was running down, the party was over and it was time to go. Saul was a farmer and farming was real. Besides which, I found him a very attractive man. I thought I was pretty lucky when I married him.'

'How long did it take you to discover he was dotty?' There were better ways of making the point, but why bother? Wives who spend their evenings helping husbands build a funeral pyre must know that theirs is a minority sport.

Lucy laughed with something approaching gaiety. 'It's subjective, isn't it? I mean, thousands of wives think it quite normal to have husbands who devote almost the whole of their spare time trying to poke a small ball into a four-inch hole. Some men spend thousands of pounds rearing birds in order that their friends may kill them. Saul just happens to admire his ancestors so much that he wants to live like them. Well, die like them anyway.'

'Does he know about Mrs Penney?'

Lucy nodded. 'Yes, I told him. He knows I give her enough money to keep herself comfortable, but he's not madly interested. He thinks what happened to her served her right for having anything to do with Americans. Only to be fair, it's not just Americans he hates—it's any foreigner who looks like settling in England. In his eyes they're all invaders.'

I said, 'It's not very logical. The Saxons weren't the original Britons. They were invaders themselves.'

'I know,' Lucy said. 'But people with bees in their bonnets aren't terribly logical, are they?'

I said, 'Neither are murderers, come to that.'

'For God's sake!' She stared at me wide-eyed. For the first time I think I'd stirred her out of her cosy acceptance of her life at Wendal Fen. 'Angus, you're not seriously suggesting that Saul could have killed Frank Segal?'

I said brutally, 'Why not? He smashed Darren Penney's hand, didn't he? The crowd in the pub knew that the squire would dole out whatever retribution he thought fit, which was why nobody would press charges at the time. I expect the wretched boy even presented himself for punishment.' I paused. 'It's true, isn't it?'

'No, of course it isn't!'

'For God's sake, woman, you know it's true!'

Lucy looked sick. 'I—I suppose it could be.'

I said, 'Then look at your husband through a policeman's eyes. Here's a man who's so divorced from reality that half of the time he really believes he's some kind of barbaric Saxon chieftain, meting out brutal justice as he thinks fit. A man who thinks it perfectly reasonable to spend most of his spare time planning the kind of bizarre death rite that hasn't been practised in this country for a thousand years. And incidentally, a man who is well known for his unreasoning hatred of foreigners, Americans in particular.'

Lucy Hayward was staring at me as though she didn't believe what she was hearing, but then it's one of the perks of a policeman's office that he's allowed to be a four-letter man at regular intervals.

'All right,' I said, 'that's the kind of man the law sees. That's the kind of man *I* see. And when I consider that Frank Segal was not only an American but a man who abandoned you as a child I have to say that I think it very likely that your husband killed him.'

She looked at me appealingly. 'Suppose I told you that I know for certain Saul didn't shoot Frank—'

I said, 'I'm sorry, Lucy, but I don't see how that can be possible.'

'Oh yes, it is.' Her voice was hardly above a whisper. 'I know Saul didn't shoot Frank, because I did.'

CHAPTER 11

If I learned anything during my years as a copper it was that one treats all confessions with a certain circumspection, based on the premise that people who break the law only admit to doing so when there's something in it for them. It wasn't particularly profound but I thought about it most of the way to the *Bell* at Felden, which was further to go for dinner than I'd intended.

I had found the place in the local Yellow Pages so there was no one to blame but myself when it turned out to be a one-time pub that avaricious brewers had done over with a wealth of glass-fibre beams and pink electric candles. I had not driven twenty miles to eat microwaved this and that with my feet in shag pile carpet, and found myself muttering to that effect.

Laurie said truthfully, 'Well, it was you who wanted to eat out.'

'I had to get out of that place.' It was true, I was getting a thing about the fen and Hayward's farm, to say nothing of Hayward's wife. Even an hour spent in an ill-conceived gin palace on the A48 was better than suffering the curious sensation of enmity that had been mine for the past couple of days. Not by nature one of the world's laughing boys, I was aware I'd been less jolly than usual. I said, 'You realize we could be here for another week?'

'You'll learn to love it by then.' She stared down at her plate. 'What am I supposed to be eating?'

'They call it a warm salad.'

'It's disgusting.'

'It's £5.50,' I told her. 'And so far as starters go, it's a bargain. Golden melon wrapped in wafer thin Parma ham and masked with a delicate gooseberry sauce would have set us back twice that.'

'Not us. You.' Laurie put the chef's offering aside. 'What are you going to do about Lucy? Arrest her?'

I said, 'I told her if she still felt the same way about it I'd take her down the station and we'd have a statement from her in the morning.'

'You're not exactly falling over yourself.'

'I'm not exactly convinced.'

'But you say she showed you the gun. That's pretty conclusive, surely?'

'She produced a .22 and a packet of long cartridges, which at the moment I've got locked in the boot.' I waited while the waiter took away one lot of awful food and brought another. When he'd retired I went on, 'The ballistics people can check if the weapon's the same. I imagine it is.'

'And she says she did it.'

'That's what she says, but no, I'm not sure.' Was I not? It's easy to accept the confession of some pimply yob caught in the act, less so when it's from someone you like. And yet—'She says she's always hated Frank Segal for having enjoyed all the things that rightly belonged to her father. Not just for pinching his wife, but for everything. Not least for talking him into taking that mission to Germany. She lost her father through Frank Segal's persuasive powers. Lost her mother, too, come to that.'

Laurie said, 'All right, lover. So what are you worrying about?'

'I suppose,' I said, 'because it seems a long time to keep resentment on the boil. I can imagine Lucy murdering Frank when she first heard the news. I can imagine her *wanting* to shoot him when she heard how he'd cashed in on her father's sporting achievements. But I can't see her brooding over it for forty years!'

'Maybe she's got a long memory.'

I said, 'Maybe. But if you're going to assume Lucy killed Frank Segal, then you've got to believe she tried to blow me up on the golf course the other day. It's almost unknown for a woman to commit murder with a rifle, let alone a grenade booby-trap. And anyway, Darren Penney was the mad bomber. The brains, anyway.'

Laurie stared at me, gratifyingly playing Watson to my Sherlock Holmes. 'How on earth do you know that?'

'In general,' I said, 'because it just seems likely. Darren would blame me for what Hayward did to him. And considering his passion for war relics it would be surprising if he hadn't got hold of a grenade or two. But in particular I know because Sergeant Davidson frightened the truth out of some pal of Darren's who was hauled in to do the actual construction work, there being only one pair of serviceable hands between the two of them.'

'So what will happen to them?'

I'd wondered that myself. I said, 'I gather Davidson would like to handle the matter unofficially. Nothing to do with me, thank God, and I'm not laying charges. But reverting to Lucy: No, she didn't shoot the Albatross.'

'But she thinks Saul Hayward did.'

'I know,' I said. 'I know. She confessed to save her husband.' It was straight out of any TV soap opera you cared to mention, but this time it seemed likely to be true. Maybe Saul hadn't killed Segal and Lucy simply thought he had. It was an interesting variation.

Laurie said, 'What happens to people who do that kind of thing? Is it an offence to make a false confession?'

'It depends,' I told her. 'Largely on the amount of trouble it's caused. Or how calculated it is. If it's just a kind of spur of the moment emotional thing we tend to forget it, but strictly it's obstructing the course of justice and so on.'

'So what are you going to do about it?'

Looking at her, it was hard to tell if she was for or agin. 'Frankly,' I said, 'I'm damned if I know.'

It hadn't been much of a meal and the bill the waiter brought me while Laurie was in the cloakroom was as bad as I'd expected, borne by a cheeky little sod who'd have been better employed cleaning out one of the local pig-pens but who was obviously going places in the catering trade.

'Has sir been here before?' Accent sort of Midlands, with a trace of something else I couldn't place. From the way he spoke to the staff I put him down as the assistant manager, but bosses are getting younger every day. A Dr Harold.

No, I told him, sir had not been here before. Sir refrained from saying that neither would he be here again.

'Perhaps you didn't know, sir, but we also have rooms.'

'Rooms?'

'Ah . . . bedrooms, sir.'

I said unhelpfully, 'Don't most inns?'

'Well, yes, of course.' He thought that one over. 'As a matter of fact, my father used to keep the *Swallow* by the old airfield at Wendal. A tiny place but even that had a couple of rooms.' He did his best to get back to his subject. 'Of course our accommodation is of a higher standard altogether.'

I said, 'I'm sure it's pleasant.' Pompous, but what the hell else was I supposed to say?

Mr Harold was busy scribbling my receipt. 'Some customers find them convenient. For changing, you understand. If they're going on somewhere. We actually call them Convenience Rooms. We have a special short term rate for them, of course.'

Well, I suppose there wasn't much else to do in the fens. 'You want to watch it,' I told him. 'Before now people have lost their licence for being too convenient.'

Mr Harold gave me a reassuring smile. 'Believe me, squire—'

I said, 'I'm not a squire. I'm a Detective-Inspector and I've just eaten a very overpriced meal, so watch it, sonny.'

So out into the night with a flourish. Bully Boy Straun strikes again. Not much good at catching killers but red hot with pimping waiters.

Laurie joined me. 'You're very quiet all of a sudden.'

I started to unlock the car. 'The head waiter was asking if he could fix us up with a short-time room.'

'Angus, he wasn't!' All eyes and ears, obviously the best thing I'd said all evening.

'I kid you not.'

'He must have thought we were—well, you know.'

'No, tell me,' I said.

'Don't be an oaf.' Laurie stared into mid distance. 'Do you remember that old Lelouche film where the couple are having dinner and Yves Montand just says to the waiter, "Have you got a room?" without even taking his eyes off the girl?'

'It was *Un Homme et Une Femme*,' I said. 'The French go along with that sort of thing.' She was still looking into mid distance. 'You don't mean you—'

'Oh, I don't know.' Laurie ducked into the car. 'I've never been taken upstairs in the middle of dinner.'

'There's time yet,' I said. But of course there wasn't.

I drove back to Wendal with a light foot. There was nothing on the road but it wasn't the kind of evening that made one want to hurry. Night comes slowly to the fen country at that time of year. The land that hasn't welcomed strangers during the day has even less time for them with the going of the light, but the huge sky was wonderful. I watched the horizon change from blue to green and then to a dull glowing red. A skein of geese headed for wherever they parked themselves for the night, and their faint cries of mutual encouragement drifted down over the mutter of the car.

Laurie said, 'What are you smiling about?'

I shook my head. I wasn't sure, but I knew I felt better than when we went out. The edge of Wendal village loomed up out of the evening mist. Over to the right was the edge of the old airfield where Smith and his crowd hung out. Further off, at what I judged to be the edge of the fen, the mist flowed with a curious incandescent light. I said, 'What do you suppose is going on there?'

Laurie leaned across me. That close, I caught her scent. Odd how erotic familiar things can be, I wondered what it was. Typical of me that I shouldn't know. Patrick Smith would have known were he in my place. Patrick Smith probably knew anyway, damn him. Laurie said, 'It looks like a floodlight. Do you suppose they're still looking for that plane?'

'They must be out of their minds if they are,' I said. 'They know that what they're doing is illegal. Why draw attention to it?'

'Perhaps it's something else.'

'We'll go and look.' Uncharitable, because even if he reckoned I wouldn't split on him, Smith was hardly likely to welcome me there. Though what could they be doing at this hour, for God's sake?

I turned in at the gate at the bottom of the old airfield and took the perimeter track to Smith's hangar. The big corrugated iron building loomed up like the side of a cliff, with not a light shining anywhere, so I skirted it and we headed for the edge of the fen where Whitton had been drowned. The glow in the sky grew stronger.

'Christ,' I said, 'they've got a searchlight or something. They must be out of their minds.' I suppose I simply took it for granted that they were still looking for the crashed Liberator and the idea didn't please me all that much. I might be prepared to forget I was a policeman once, but it seemed a bit much that I should be expected to turn my back twice on their fun and games. Nobody likes to be ignored. Neither does one want to be over-zealous. All the same, if they'd got that plane up and the crew were still in it there was going to be a certain amount of hell to pay.

'Whatever they're doing,' Laurie said, 'they're making enough noise about it.'

She was right as usual. As I slowed the car one could hear the high whine of a motor. I remembered the track to the fen and nosed between the reeds towards it. No more than a few hundred yards and it opened out so that one could see the water, like ink in the half light. The Maserati's headlights bored over the two Land-Rovers parked at the water's edge, the figure of a man standing with his back to us and, in the mid distance, Smith's ex-War Department salvage barge throbbing under the efforts of its winch. Someone had raised a kind of boom, so that it was drawing in a steel cable at an angle of forty-five degrees, a giant's fishing rod outlined against the mauve sky.

I switched off the car's lights and got out. Behind me Laurie sighed. 'Oh dear, they've really got something. Let's just be tactful and go.'

'Stop sounding like the great British public,' I told her. Whatever it was on the end of the cable was half obscured by the figure in front of me, but I glimpsed the hard outlines of some kind of framework. I thought for a moment that it was the intricate pattern of a geodetic airframe but then I remembered that it was a B-24 that had gone into the fen and not a Wellington.

'Oh God, Angus,' Laurie whispered. 'Can't you see what it is?'

But at that moment I was more interested in the man in front of me. I don't know why, but I'd assumed it to be Smith and it had puzzled me that he hadn't turned round when I'd caught him in my headlights. Now I saw that it wasn't Smith but Saul Hayward, unaware of me or anyone else. He was staring out towards the salvage barge with the kind of expression Galahad must have had when he glimpsed the Holy Grail. His mouth worked and suddenly he raised his arms towards the sky.

'Oh gods, I thank you!'

'Hayward!' I grabbed his shoulder and gave him a shake, probably not the recommended treatment for someone in a state of ecstasy but effective enough. He dropped his arms and turned towards me without noticeable embarrassment and said conversationally, 'You see, the offering was acceptable. First the offering, then the reward.'

I said roughly, 'Pull yourself together. What the devil are you talking about?'

'By Odin, Straun! Look for yourself!' He gestured out over the fen. I looked. Now he was out of the way I could see better what Smith and his crew were pulling out of the water. The broken and blackened spars that projected above the water weren't part of an airframe. For a moment the pattern didn't mean anything to me at all and then all of a sudden the penny dropped and I saw the spars as a keel and strakes and the long, upward-curving sweep of a bow.

I said, 'It's some old boat.'

'Some old boat! *Some* old boat!' My words seemed to have brought on a sort of frenzy. 'It's not just some old boat, you dolt! It's Morcar the Left-Handed's funeral ship. Back after more than a thousand years!'

CHAPTER 12

You're supposed to get just about anything in this life if you try long and hard enough. The trouble is that by the time it arrives the situation's changed.

'A boat!' Chief Superintendent Higham was saying over the phone. 'A *funeral* boat?'

I said, 'It's what the ancient Saxons—'

Higham was in Lincoln but he didn't really need the phone. 'I know what a funeral boat is, dammit. I just want to know what this farmer of yours is doing with one.'

'He hasn't got one,' I said. 'He just thinks he has.' It was my own fault, I should have taken the day off and sorted it out face to face. But start a thing and there's no going back. 'I've seen the thing they've dredged up. It's the remains of some kind of wherry. A hundred years old at most.'

'Living out his fantasies, eh?'

'Yes.' Why pay a shrink when you can do it yourself?

'And you're happy the wife's in the clear?'

I said, 'She didn't kill Segal, that's for sure.'

'So it was all an accident. Wrap it up, Straun. Get on home.'

Well, what was I waiting for? It was what I'd been waiting for long enough, but now I'd got my green light some niggling qualm held me back. I said, 'You were going to get me something out about this chap Smith.'

'The aircraft buff?'

'Yes,' I said. 'Him.'

'Nothing known.' I felt a twinge of disappointment. I suppose somewhere at the back of my mind I'd had an ungenerous thought that he'd done time for drug-trafficking, running a disorderly house and driving with his alcohol count .0005 of a milligram above the legal level. Higham went on, 'Ex-regular army. Plenty of family money. Well known in the trade, so to speak. Something of an authority on old planes.'

Well, it made a change from old cars. I wondered how much I'd lose on the Maserati if I tried to sell it now. Well, horses for courses. I said, 'I'll stay another couple of days.'

'Must you?'

'Hayward's giving a party,' I said. 'It's to coincide with Smith flying his plane out. I thought I'd stay for it.'

'Well, it's on your own time.'

'Yes, sir,' I said. 'I'll remember that.' I wondered if he thought I was going to send him a bill.

CHAPTER 13

The man on the radio said that there would be good weather for Saul's party, and when I drew back the curtains and had a look I guessed he must have done the same thing because he'd got it right. Mist was lying low over the fields as usual, and the three or four cows in the next field were standing hock high in the stuff, but the sky was the all-over pale grey that in Lincolnshire means that there's a fifty-fifty chance of it not raining. Laurie came out of the bath in a towelling robe and phoney good cheer to cover the fact that she'd spent the night in her room and I in mine.

I said, 'It looks as though Saul's going to have a good day for his party.'

She gave me a sisterly peck. 'He'd be cross with his Norse gods if it wasn't.' Why was the ice so thin? Why was she so bloody-minded about Smith? Why did I feel so bad about Lois? Come to that, what the hell was wrong with us that we couldn't get ourselves sorted out? She said, 'People will think he's out of his mind, lashing out free drink because of a boat that isn't even on show.'

I said, 'It's probably just as well, since most of them would know an old wherry when they saw one.' Only they weren't going to get the chance because Saul had insisted on lowering the old wreck back into the water 'to preserve the timbers', which must have been a spot of expertise he'd picked up from the *National Geographic*. Did Saul really think that those bits of wood were a thousand years old, or did he just want them to be? Which was just another way of asking oneself if the man was barking mad or simply letting his enthusiasm get a bit out of hand.

Laurie frowned. 'What shall I wear?'

'Any damn thing you like.' I sometimes forgot that Laurie was essentially an urban soul, curiously out of her depth in the country. 'People don't dress up for this kind of party. All Saul means is that the drinks are on him. The *Packet Boat* will be masterminding the bar, Barney Summers told me so yesterday.'

'Will there be a village band?'

'I don't know. Possibly.' My own experience of rural junkets was limited to ones north of the border which could hardly be said to count, and the pastoral shindigs I'd come upon in the way of business. Wellies and duffel coats with straw bales to sit on seemed to be the general form. I said, 'Anyway, don't start thinking it's going to be like the North of England Show. People are thin on the ground round here. My guess is Saul is going to get half a dozen nosey neighbours who hope he's going to make a fool of himself and a hard core of *Packet Boat* regulars on the track of free drink.'

One makes all these wild statements which experience should have taught usually turn out to be wrong, but on this occasion I got away with it. The vintage aircraft movement could well have scented the excitement from afar and turned up in droves to see a B-24 in action for real, but by the time we got down to the hangar, which was about eleven, *Liberty Belle* was still sitting at the entrance to her hangar and the only bit of my prediction that seemed to be working out was the eager crowd round the trestle tables that Barney had erected beside the runway as a makeshift bar.

Laurie gave a quick glance round and said, 'You were right! I do think that was clever of you.' She was wearing green boots and one of those heavy Aran sweaters with a high collar and she looked as though she'd been a life member of the CPRE. Among the dozen or so local farmers' wives and the odd professional couple she was spot on and happily aware of the fact. I had the comfortable feeling of getting something right for a change.

'There is a band, too,' Laurie said. 'How did you know?' It was a small jazz combo that probably made the round of the local village halls on Saturday nights, guitar, keyboard and drums. I watched while they rigged up their primitive amplification gear and started to beat out something that sounded not unlike St James Infirmary Blues. Jack Keating came by, flying jacket over his arm.

''Morning, Mr Straun. Come to see us off?'

'We have indeed.' I nodded at the well nigh empty space behind the hangar. 'I thought you might have had a few vintage plane people along for the take-off.'

'Oh, they only turn up at air shows. Not worth the trip for a single plane.'

'No,' I said, 'I suppose not. Where's the pilot?'

Keating shook his head. 'Dunno, Mr Straun. In the hangar, I expect.'

'Well, thanks for fixing the car, anyway.'

'The car?' Keating looked blank, then collected himself. 'Oh, sure, the car. You're welcome.' He nodded and I saw him switch off at the same time. He forgot me, forgot the business of the car. Just hitched his jacket up under his arm and went on his way.

'Darling,' Laurie said, 'you shouldn't. The poor man's got other things on his mind besides Maseratis.'

'Yes,' I said, 'I expect he has. Look, there's a worthy woman over there selling raffle tickets. Go and buy some. I'll be back in a minute.'

'You *want* raffle tickets?'

'No,' I told her, 'but go and buy some.'

I walked over to the hangar. Smith was in one corner, dwarfed by a huge wing, his back to me as he bent over the big trestle table he used as a desk. Someone, probably Keating, called to him, and he straightened up, threw down his pencil and went out past the nose of the aircraft to somewhere in front of the hangar.

I walked over to the desk with no other intention than to wait for him; at the most I wanted to wish him good luck. And let's face it, I would be glad to see him go. I stood for a moment, waiting for him, not really seeing the map in front of me but not not seeing it either. I supposed it was *Liberty Belle's* flight plan. A neat pencilled cross by Wendal Fen, a pencilled line to the base at West Canby to take on fuel, then west across England, the Irish Sea to Dublin, presumably for a final top-up before heading out over the Atlantic.

I looked up at the vast wing above me, the swell of the two port engine housings and the massive tricycle undercarriage holding the thing up. B-24s had a range of at least three thousand miles. Three thousand miles in terms of aviation fuel was a lot of gallons. I wondered, in the manner of non-flying folk, how something weighing Heaven knows how many tons managed to stay up there in the air. McInroe, standing at the hatch, studied me impassively, ruminating, I supposed, on the gulf fixed between those who can't and those who can. Smith didn't seem to be showing signs of returning so I drifted back to where Saul was standing in front of a blackboard on which he'd pinned an ancient map of East Anglia and from what I could hear was trying to drum up the interest of half a dozen locals in their Saxon heritage.

'—of course Harold was a splendid chap, but lucky. If William of Normandy hadn't visited England in '52 people might never have cottoned on to the fact he wanted the place for himself. But as it was, the Witan got uneasy and ordered their lands restored to Godwin's sons. Harold got the earldom of the West Saxons that way. Mind you, wouldn't have got it if his brother Sweyn hadn't died on a pilgrimage—'

I watched his audience shuffle their feet, an innate cour-
tesy preventing them from drifting away too soon. And I
suppose it counted that he was the squire. Squire was
entitled to ramble on if he felt like it. Saxons, earldoms,
Witan bounced unnoticed off their tolerant skulls. Laurie,
at the back of the group, caught my eye.

'The man's obsessed!'

I said, 'So are people about football, but I suppose it
doesn't do any harm.' But I wasn't all that sure. Dotty
over one thing, not exactly bright over another. Yet Saul
certainly didn't show any sign of being altogether ninety
cents in the dollar, not with the most successful farm for
miles around. I towed her away regardless to a stall where
an amiable lady sold us coffee and biscuits. A few yards
away the local Women's Institute were doing a brisk trade
in homemade preserves while half a dozen beady-eyed
traders were already flogging junk from the backs of their
cars to a background of St Louis Blues. All in all, it was
taking on the look and feel of a rustic celebration. Back in
Shakespeare's time, Bottom the Weaver would have been
doing his thing, too.

Bang!

I winced as 1200 horsepower of Pratt and Whitney radial
engine whined, spat, coughed a bit and then exploded in
raucous life. After a few moments a second started up, then
a third.

'Sounds good, boy, dunnit?' Barney Summers at my side,
sniffing the scent of exhaust fumes. He was wearing his
usual lumberjack's shirt, with its sleeves incongruously
rolled down to the cuffs, a thatch of grey hair sprouting out
of the unbuttoned front, more a farmer than most of the
people around.

I said, 'Who's looking after your bar?'

'I've got a couple of lads who help out.' He limped round

me like a good-tempered Quasimodo. 'Would you and your lady like a drop, now?'

'A bit later, thanks, Barney.' I don't suppose he heard me because they'd got the plane out on the apron and were running the engines up till the earth shook. A sort of horizontal cyclone of dust, chopped straw and whatever goes to make up the surface junk of a farm field swirled and blasted back among the crowd. Abruptly the engines were cut back and the subsequent quiet was almost deafening. I looked at the huge tailplanes through the open-ended hangar and the sun touched polished metal till it flashed fire. I thought uncharitably that running classic motorcars was expensive enough, just feeding fuel to a bomber wouldn't bear thinking about.

I think Barney must have read my thoughts because he grinned and shook his head. 'Must cost a fortune, that lot. Just as well he never had a wife, eh boy?'

Laurie frowned. 'He did have a wife.'

Not according to Higham he hadn't. Though, come to think of it, he'd never specifically mentioned one at all. I looked at Laurie. 'How do you know?'

'Because he told me. He had two children, too.'

I said, 'Had? You never told me. What happened to them?'

'They were killed. All three of them.' She stopped abruptly and I saw her face flush red. Odd, I'd never seen her do that before. She said, 'Oh shit. I wasn't supposed to tell.'

'God damn it,' I said. '*How were they killed?*'

Laurie blinked. 'It was while Patrick was serving in Ireland. The IRA put a bomb under his car, but he wasn't using it for some reason. His wife decided to take the children shopping in it instead.'

Oddly, it was the least important thing that flashed through my mind first—the fact that no vintage plane buffs had turned up that morning to see the only airworthy B-24 in the country actually airborne. But Smith wouldn't have told anybody. And then, and only then, did I remember the flight plan, with its tiny pencilled diversion to Dublin.

Liberty Belle's engines speeded up again, like a signal. I felt the company man's moment of panic, when life parts company with the book. There's nothing wrong with the police training, all in all pretty good, although largely based on back-up of one sort or another. No bad thing, discouraging gung-ho factions apt to plunge in regardless, but how does one leave last words behind one when things go wrong? No words from Heaven came down to tell me, so I dropped my cup of coffee over my feet and ran.

How far was it to the *Liberty Belle*? A hundred yards? Whatever it was, I covered it smartish. Running through the wash of the propellers was like going through an invisible wall but I just kept my head down and kept going. I looked up once to see Barney Summers walking towards me. He stopped dead and looked at me curiously. 'Something the matter, then?'

I said, 'Help me stop Smith. That plane's got a full bomb load.'

I might have expected the landlord of the *Packet Boat* to look blank at that kind of remark but he didn't. Perhaps he saw something in my face that scared him, because without my saying anything he started running with me, in his curious shambling trot.

I got abreast of *Liberty Belle*'s tailplane, took in the fact that Keating was still on sentry go beside the hatch. An amiable sentry, smiling at his boss's mad friend.

I mouthed, 'I want to see Smith,' and pointed towards the hatch. Keating couldn't have heard me above the thunder of the motors but he got the idea all right. I saw the smile wipe off his face as if it had never been there and he

shook his head, jerking his hand forward in a flat No Go
gesture.

I pushed him aside. As a policeman it's fairly easy to
push people aside in what is light-heartedly known as the
course of duty. Less easy when the pushed pulls out one of
those frightening US army issue Colt automatics with a
bore big enough to fire marbles. I'd no desire at all to
discover what it felt like to be shot by one of those things,
so I took a running kick at the point where it seemed likely
to hurt him most. The great advantage of dirty fighting is
that defence against it is purely instinctive. Once a man
knows that a boot is on a collision course with his genitals
his thought processes simply surrender themselves to a
series of reflexes, which is what happened to Keating.
Entirely of their own volition his thighs clamped coyly
together and his hips twisted the lower part of his body
sideways. He didn't exactly stand on one leg but so far as
his balance was concerned he might as well have done,
because at that point Barney Summers's fist caught him on
the side of the jaw and knocked him flat.

I'd have laughed if I'd had time, but by then things were
beginning to move uncomfortably fast. *Liberty Belle* was
moving forward at a brisk clip and I made a grab at the
open hatch with my nearest arm. Unfortunately it happened to be the one that had taken most of the blast of a
bank robber's sawn-off shotgun many a year gone. Playing
golf with it is dodgy, trying to haul oneself into a moving
plane with it dodgier still, and for a moment I truly thought
the thing was about to be torn off. I screamed, and even
though he couldn't possibly have heard me over the racket
of the motors Barney must have realized that something
was wrong. With surprising agility for so clumsy a man he
snatched at the edge of the hatch and hauled himself into
the aircraft with almost nonchalant ease. A moment later
he'd twisted his massive shoulders and clamped a hairy

paw round my wrist. There's something to be said for a
lifetime of pulling beer handles. I felt as though I'd got
myself attached to a crane. Safely, if inelegantly, I found
myself beside him while below us the concrete slid past. I
pulled myself upright and looked round.

I don't know what I'd expected the interior of a B-24 to
look like. One gets used to climbing aboard aircraft and
finding the thing full of seats, each lit by a window. *Liberty
Belle* had no seats and no windows, the walls of her hull
were bare metal and rivets, so that you could see the way
she was built. You could also see that this particular B-24
might be nearly fifty years old but she could still do the job
for which she was intended. *Liberty Belle* was a bomber, and
at this moment *Liberty Belle* was carrying a full load of
bombs.

Barney and I stood and looked at the things. God knows,
they couldn't very well be missed because on the B-24 the
missiles are carried vertically in rows on either side of the
fuselage, divided by a narrow metal catwalk running up
the middle. Below and beside them were the roller shutter
doors that were wound aside before the bomb run com-
menced.

'Jesus!' Barney said. 'You were right.'

I looked up towards the nose of *Liberty Belle*. There'd
been a time when one wouldn't have been able to look
very far, with a crew of seven each doing their own thing,
bomb-aiming, turret-gunning, navigating, working the
radio or simply getting in each other's way as they readied
for the bomb run.

The bomb run. One was used to thinking of the words
in terms of a wartime target, brave clipped British voices
over the intercom in old black and white movies.

'*Bomb doors open!*'
'*Keep her steady, Skipper! Steady!*'
'*Bombs gone!*'

'Well done, Jacko! Time we were going, chaps!'

Well, that had all been a long time ago. The question was, where was a B-24 with a full 8000-pound bomb load likely to go today? Not to the Ruhr, that was for sure. Not with a pilot who'd got a major account to settle with the IRA and a course ready charted for Ireland. Simple, really. Ex-Captain Patrick Smith was about to bomb Dublin.

One could argue that the good citizens of Dublin could hardly be held responsible for the death of Smith's wife and children, but if the IRA bombed Belfast one could see a certain lunatic reasoning behind a grief-crazed mind. Probably Keating and McInroe, if one probed deep enough, would have similar stories to tell.

I poked Barney in the ribs and pointed up towards the cockpit. Unlike British aircraft, all American World War Two bombers were designed for a first and second pilot, using dual controls. Smith was up there by himself, in the left-hand seat, and it was just possible to see the back of his right shoulder through the opening in the forward bulkhead. From where I stood I got a fair view of the right-hand control column moving fractionally in unison with Smith's, the big block of dials over the radio operator's tiny desk. We had the place to ourselves. Two of us to cope with one maniac sitting with his back to us, intent on taxi-ing gently up the runway. As our fathers would have said, a piece of cake.

Well, it would have been if Barney hadn't tripped over one of the drilled formers that held the fuselage together and landed flat on his face.

I doubt if Smith heard him fall, there was too much noise from the engines for that, but he must have felt the impact because he glanced over his shoulder. It was a glance that took in Barney, then flicked up to me. There was no surprise in his eyes, only awareness. I suppose a combination of army training and a passion for flying must have sharpened his reaction times because having once registered we were there he didn't hang about. He simply turned his back on us and I saw his right hand smack down on the grouped throttle controls and ram them forward. The Pratt and Whitneys bellowed and *Liberty Belle* shuddered under a vast surge of torque even at the same moment as the aircraft began to accelerate.

Four-thousand-odd horsepower provides a good deal of get up and go even for something the size and weight of a B-24. *Liberty Belle* shook a bit but she lifted her skirts and fairly fled out on to the long straight of Wendal Fen's remaining runway. There being no seat-belts to fasten, the thrust brought the two of us to our knees again, painful on a floor all sharp edges. By the time we were up and moving forward again *Liberty Belle* must have been travelling at about eighty miles an hour and rising. I had no notion of the ground speed at which a fully laden B-24 gets unstuck but I did have a gut feeling that this was no time to interfere with the driver.

That was something Smith must have realized because he didn't give us a second glance. Barney and I stood behind him like a couple of lemons while the engines took up that special throbbing harmony that announces the fact one is about to become airborne. The wheels left the concrete, hit it again, bounced clear and *Liberty Belle*'s nose tilted upwards and the old girl was up and away.

I hung on to a convenient bit of hardware and cursed Smith's quick thinking. According to Straun's traveller's guide, it's OK to complain to the steward but nobody in their right mind messes with the pilot. Who else is going to keep twelve tons of aircraft in the air?

I looked about me, a stranger in these parts. A wartime bomber and a modern jet of the same size have really only flight in common. *Liberty Belle* was probably as tight and secure as craftsmanship could make her, nevertheless the vibration and noise had to be experienced to be believed, like living in a tin can full of bolts.

Smith brought up the undercarriage. We could hear the whine of the motor and the thump as the wheels tucked themselves away in their nacelles. Among the dials on the packed instrument board a red light went out. Smith looked at me and smiled.

'You coming along for the ride?' In the cockpit, ahead of the whirling propellers, it was marginally quieter, I suppose because we were ahead of the noise. Smith had to shout but one could understand him all right.

'Go back while you've got the chance.'

Smith missed what I was saying and made a gesture of irritation. I don't think he cared very much whether he heard me or not but I suppose like most madmen he wanted to be sure I heard him, because he picked up one of those World War Two leather helmets ready wired for in-plane sound. He pulled it on and pointed to the one on the radio operator's table beside me. I put the thing on too, feeling like something in *Twelve o'Clock High*.

I said, 'Smith, don't be a fool. Turn back.'

'On the contrary.' Smith's voice crackled unnaturally in my ears. 'If I land you may find some way of stopping me. Up here you've got no option but to leave me alone.'

'Do you honestly think it'll do any good to bomb Dublin? God knows how many women and children—'

Smith raised his eyebrows. 'So you worked that out, did you? Well, the Irish Republican Army are pretty good at killing women and children. Killed mine, anyway, and plenty more besides. They're always saying that they're at war, because they know the politicians make damn sure our boys fight with one arm tied behind their backs. The IRA have had a ball bombing Belfast whenever they felt like it. Now their precious capital's going to find out how it feels to be on the receiving end for a change.'

I said, 'The RAF will shoot you down before you get there.'

'Who's going to tell them?'

Liberty Belle lurched as she hit a bump and I watched the sureness of Smith's hands as he brought her back. He was right, of course. He'd have filed his flight plan and he wouldn't have to divert from it till the last minute. I wondered how he was going to cope without a bomb aimer, but then I remembered the way he looked that last time I'd seen him on the ground. It had puzzled me at the time but now I remembered photographs of Japanese pilots taken before they set off on their one-way flights. Smith's face had had the same look about it and I realized that one way or another he wasn't intending to come back. He was going to crash his bomb-laden plane into the heart of a busy city.

His voice broke in on my thoughts. 'If you don't mind using a parachute I won't insist on you coming all the way.'

I said, 'You bloody maniac, go back!'

Smith laughed. He was still laughing when I hooked my good left arm round his neck and my not so good right hand under his armpit. Anger is always a plus in matters of brute strength and when I jammed one foot against the back of his seat and pulled, he came out over the back of it almost like a child. It happened so quickly that I fell over backwards with Smith on top of me, which wasn't as planned but I think he was so startled that he wasn't thinking properly and I managed to get to my feet first. He wasn't far behind me, though, and he lashed out and caught me in the ribs before I smashed him twice across the side of his jaw. His head rocked sideways and smacked rather nastily against a drilled metal spar. I saw Smith's eyes go out of focus and blood well up and run across his temple before his knees sagged and he folded up at my feet.

Liberty Belle hit an air pocket or something and jolted alarmingly, like a horse who senses its rider is no longer in control. The unmanned control column dipped and swayed and when I tore my glance away it was to find Barney Summers staring from the motionless Smith to me, his eyes wide.

I waved towards the empty pilot seat, shouting to make myself heard. 'Well, don't just stand there, Captain Bazil. Fly the bloody thing!'

CHAPTER 14

Barney did as he was told. Not strictly Barney, but Barney to me. He shuffled crabwise into the pilot's seat and grabbed the stubby half-wheel with the Ford badge in the boss. It had been a long time since he'd flown a B-24 but the trick didn't seem to have left him. I felt the deck steady beneath my feet, then tilt as he began the wide circle back the way we'd come. I hoped he hadn't lost his touch when it came to landing, because there were too many bombs on board for me to feel happy about them bouncing about. Come to think of it, one bomb would be more than enough. I'd have said so to my pilot but he hadn't got a headset and I didn't want to take his mind off the job by shouting at him, so I sat down on the flight engineer's stool and waited to see what happened.

Not long to wait. The front screens of the B-24 didn't give much of a view forward, unnerving to the passenger who is apt to think that the pilot can see where he's going, but it was comforting to note that Barney seemed content enough to peer out over the side, nor did he fumble his way round the controls. He was captain of the ship all right. I felt the aircraft lurch as the flaps came on and the pitch of the bellowing engines change in the moments before the huge wheels touched back on the ground, then the sharp squark of the brakes and the trundling rumble of tyres that precedes a stop. Barney hauled himself slowly out of his seat, the propellers turning over gently.

I nodded towards Smith, still out cold. 'You'd better give me a hand with him.'

Barney nodded without speaking, seized Smith by the collar and began to drag him towards the rear of the plane.

It wasn't an easy trip for someone on his own because the aircraft was built on two levels and reaching the hatch involved a flight of steps. Dragging an unconscious third party from flight deck down to the bomb bay catwalk made it almost absurdly difficult and I tried to picture what it must have been like keeping a B-24 flying back from Germany with half the crew dead and an engine on fire. I couldn't, which was perhaps just as well, but the idea made me less concerned about Smith and we reached the lower hatch at last.

Barney opened the hatch, with its skimpy few rungs of aluminium ladder, and grabbed Smith by the shoulders. To me he said, 'You'd better go first and grab him, otherwise he'll break his neck.'

'Well, make sure you let him down feet first,' I said. I was half way down the steps when something—probably Barney's boot—caught me between the shoulders and I landed flat on my face on the concrete.

Had I thought of anything it would have been that I'd fallen for the oldest trick in the business, but for a few minutes I was too stunned to think of anything apart from the fact that my head hurt where it had scraped on the ground. By the time I'd staggered to my feet the ladder had gone and the hatch was clamped shut.

'Barney!' I shouted. 'Don't be a fool!' He didn't hear me, of course. I couldn't hear myself because the engines had speeded up with a roar and the prop wash caught me unprepared and knocked me flat again. By the time I'd got up for a second time *Liberty Belle* was already gathering speed. I'd been dropped almost out of sight of the hangar and any other human being, so I just stood there and watched the old aircraft growing smaller as it hammered its way back into the air. Dust and loose bits of this and that blasted back and swirled round me but I stayed where I was, watching for the moment when the wings began to rock and you could see daylight under the hull.

Liberty Belle cleared the hangar with what looked like about ten feet to spare and I saw the wheels start to go up. Where did the man think he was going? Smith might have made it across the Atlantic, but Barney wasn't likely to after nearly fifty years. And even Smith wouldn't have attempted to fly a B-24 any distance single-handed.

The two big tail fins were hardly discernible now, but the aircraft didn't seem to be gaining height. I thought I detected a break in the engine note but at that distance it was hard to be sure. But then I knew that *Liberty Belle* wasn't holding her height. A few moments before and she'd been above the distant outline of willows, now she had dipped below them. Disappeared. I just stood there and waited, and for quite a long time I thought that perhaps everything was going to be all right. Then the sound of the motors wasn't there any more, just a silence and a great flash of light and after what seemed an age there was a vast pall of smoke and an explosion that seemed to shake the earth.

CHAPTER 15

I knew it was Todhunter as soon as the phone rang, the sixth sense the fox uses to give him advance warning that the stirrup cup is being passed around.

'Angus, dear boy, it's Adrian here.' I was not his dear boy and I scented trouble with the first name bit.

'Yes,' I said. 'It was quite a bang. Not much harm done, though. Grosvenor Square can relax.'

'I understand it was an American aircraft.' Adrian Todhunter lived with a built-in panic factor that was activated by virtually anything that could cause unhappiness between Them and Us. There were times when he tempted me to start a small war, just for the fun of the thing. On the other hand, there were limits.

'The aircraft was made in the United States,' I told him. 'But owned by an Englishman named Smith.'

'You're sure?'

'Yes,' I said. 'Quite sure.'

'But I gather there were bombs.'

I said, 'Smith was a fanatical opponent of the IRA. He was using an old wartime aircraft in what he conceived to be a retaliatory raid against Dublin. Rather fortunately the plane crashed. That's all.' Well, it was not all but it was damn all to do with Todhunter and I wasn't in the mood to indulge him more than was absolutely necessary. I added, 'We don't know about the bombs. There must have been some left behind when the airfield was abandoned.'

'Left *behind*?'

I said cheerfully, 'If you look at a plan of a bomber airfield you'll see it's by no means impossible. For one thing, they used to disperse the bombs as far away from the domestic area as possible for obvious reasons. A lot of small dumps cut the risk of accidents down a lot compared with one big one. They were sited in underground bunkers, often with grass growing over them for camouflage. If one happened to get missed when the airfield was decommissioned, I'd say it's not all that odd.'

There was the briefest pause, then Todhunter's voice said, 'Are you telling me that Smith chose Wendal as his base because he knew there were abandoned bombs there?'

'I don't know,' I told him. Nor did I. I said, 'Which came first, the chicken or the egg? We know Smith had a thing about old aircraft. Maybe he was restoring *Liberty Belle* quite innocently when he came across an old bomb dump and the idea of having his revenge on Dublin grew from there. His assistants would probably know, but they've disappeared.'

'There'll be questions in the House.'

Well, yes. The fire brigade had gone home, as had most of the locals, an explosion in water leaving remarkably little to see. But the civil air people would doubtless be along shortly, and by the time they'd made their report the Opposition politicians would be on to it all right.

Will the Minister not come clean and admit that it is a disgrace that stocks of high explosive weapons are left lying around for anyone to pick up . . .

I said comfortingly, 'Whoever was responsible has probably been dead for years. Nobody's going to be able to get much political mileage from that. With any luck the whole thing'll be forgotten in forty-eight hours.'

'I hope you're right, dear boy.' But Todhunter's voice told me that the worst was over. He added, 'And you're quite sure that no American nationals were hurt in any way?'

It took me a long time to think that one over, but not so long that Todhunter would have noticed. 'Yes, Adrian,' I said. 'Quite, quite sure.'

CHAPTER 16

I put the phone down and went back into the farmhouse kitchen, where Laurie and Lucy were sitting in front of the Aga, drinking coffee. I went over to the window and stared out at the few traces of smoke that still drifted from the spot where *Liberty Belle* had gone into the fen. Eight thousand pounds of bomb had made one hell of a bang but the plane had gone in pretty deep and much of the explosion had been dampened down by all that slush around it. As a talking point it would probably last for weeks, but apart from the odd roof getting blown off, a hen house here and there and lots of trees shedding their leaves a bit early, one couldn't say that it had done anybody much harm. Less harm than if it had fallen on Dublin, that's for sure.

I turned back and had a look at Lucy. Her face wore the chilled, breathless look of the newly bereaved but the hand clutching her coffee mug was steady. I felt sorry for her, but if she was going to lose her father his going could have been worse.

I said, 'When did you first realize that Barney Sutton was your father?'

She swallowed coffee, put the mug down on the scrubbed pine table in front of her. 'Six or seven years ago. I forget exactly.' She stared into the distance, seeing those years, I suppose. 'It sounds silly, just said like that, but I was a small child when he was shot down. I'd never known him. I no more recognized him than he did me.'

'So how did you find out?'

'Aunt Marion—Mrs Penney—told me. My father had made himself known to her but made her swear she'd keep the knowledge to herself. And I think she would have done if she hadn't caught pneumonia and thought she was going to die.'

I said, 'So she decided she'd split before she went.' It's astonishing how many people clear their conscience by breaking confidences. Or should one call them proxy confessions?

Lucy smiled faintly. 'I suppose you could say that. It must have been quite a shock to her when she discovered that she wasn't going to die after all.'

'And so you finally got together.'

'It was harder than you'd think,' Lucy said. 'We didn't know each other, we'd no background in common. We were two strangers who just happened to be father and daughter. He didn't want the news to get around. I think he'd grown so used to being Barney Summers that he didn't want to be reminded that he was really James Bazil.'

'I'm sorry,' Laurie said, 'but I don't understand. How did James Bazil become Barney Summers? Barney wasn't American. He was music-hall Lincolnshire.'

'That's just about what he was,' I told her. 'Real American, stage English rustic. He was all-American James Bazil when he was shot down over Germany in September of 1944, reported killed. That was true of the rest of the crew, but not of Bazil. He was badly knocked about but he survived. Apparently he was lucky in being found by one of the Resistance, whose members looked after him for some time. Then he tried to make his way to Spain. Someone split on him and he was picked up by the Germans. First by fighting troops, later the Gestapo.'

Laurie moved uneasily. In the 'nineties just talking about the Gestapo is an embarrassment, a mention of the unmentionable. Well, in some circles anyway. She said, 'But why the Gestapo? Why didn't they just make him a prisoner of war?'

'Because he'd been helped by the Resistance,' I told her.

'One more captured flyer was neither here nor there but the Resistance was something else again. They wanted to know about that, and Bazil could tell them.' I looked at Lucy. There are some things that are better left alone but why dodge round the things we should be proud of just because they cause us pain? I said, 'Your father didn't tell them. He was nearly a cripple when they got their hands on him, by the time they'd finished he was a wreck. But he didn't tell them what they wanted to know and he didn't die, so they shipped him off to Dachau, just to see if a concentration camp could finish what they'd begun.'

Lucy looked at me for the first time. 'But it didn't.'

A statement, not a question, and how right she was. I said, 'No, he survived. I don't think anyone knows quite how he managed it, but he did. It seems he actually *escaped* from Dachau while the fighting was still going on. He reached the Russians, who promptly threw him into another camp. After the war they discovered they'd got a slight diplomatic embarrassment on their hands and hastily sent what was left of Captain Bazil back to England. It would have been considered bad manners to make a thing of it at the time, Russia being our glorious Ally, so the whole thing was treated like a diplomatic hot potato. Someone presumably signed for one part-worn American bomber pilot and that was that.'

'You're guessing,' Lucy said.

I shook my head. 'No, you can take my word for it. He came back. He came back to Wendal. This was in 1948 or thereabouts, and there were still plenty of people who remembered the wartime days. He learned what had happened to his wife, and for some reason he decided that he didn't want to go back to his own country. He'd always liked this part of the world, perhaps it was what he'd thought about during his years as a prisoner. Whatever the reason, he decided to stay. He changed his name, got a job

He'd always been good on the stage, so it probably wasn't difficult to drop into a part permanently. I don't suppose it was all that long before everyone automatically thought of him as Barney Summers.'

Laurie said, 'I find that hard to believe.'

'Do you?' I said. 'I don't. For one thing, he didn't even remotely resemble the good-looking young officer who'd married a pretty local girl. He'd survived the destruction of his plane but his legs had been terribly injured and the fact that they never got proper treatment left him crippled. His face had been scarred too, so he wore a beard, and because the Gestapo had contributed a few hellish offerings of their own he'd come back looking like some unfortunate who'd been deformed from birth. Besides, as the years passed, the few people who remembered him began to die off or move away. I'd lay money that almost everyone in Wendal thought of Barney as Lincolnshire born and bred.'

Laurie said, 'After all this time I expect Barney did, too.'

'No,' I told her. 'Barney didn't. I don't think Barney forgot for one moment who it was who'd talked him into flying that mission in the first place. Who he had to thank for whatever ghastly things happened to him at the hands of the Gestapo, for the years in death camps, for lifelong physical pain. He'd probably accepted the fact that his wife had been no great loss, but just the same he wouldn't have been human if he hadn't pictured his good friend Al Segal tucked up in the *Swallow's* best bedroom with Eileen while German fighters were blasting his B-24 out of the sky. So when Albatross Segal actually came back in person, Barney must have felt that fate was paying him out a jackpot.'

'You really think he hated him that much?'

'Oh yes,' I said. 'That much and more. He stalked us all the time we were playing those few holes round the perimeter course, and when Segal couldn't resist going upstairs to have a last look at his love-nest he sealed his death warrant. Do you know the last thing Barney said to me up there in the plane? *Well, at least I got the son of a bitch.* And he was laughing as he said it.'

'I'm glad,' Lucy said. 'I suppose I shouldn't be, but I'm glad. My father went through hell because of that man and he deserved his vengeance, even if he did have to die for it.'

'Tell me,' I said, 'did you know it was your father who shot Segal?'

'He didn't tell me and I didn't ask him,' Lucy said. 'But yes, of course I knew. I mean, it couldn't have been anyone else, could it?'

'He didn't say anything when he gave you the rifle?'

Lucy shook her head. 'He didn't give me the rifle. I asked for it. I had some sort of idea that he might be discovered trying to get rid of it, so I thought I'd better look after it for him. He knew I used a .22 all the time shooting vermin, so I told him my own rifle had gone for repair and could he lend me his. Possibly he guessed what was in my mind but he couldn't very well refuse without telling me what he'd done.'

'Did your husband know?'

'Saul?' Lucy moved her hands in a tiny gesture. 'I'm sure he didn't. You've seen what he's like. He's one of the best farmers in the county—works hard, knows all the up to the minute things that are happening on the land development scene. But the rest of the time he's living in his own weird Saxon dream world. It was a joke when I married him, because it was just his—thing. Like golf or collecting old matchboxes. But over the years it's become almost more important than reality. Sometimes I even wonder whether in his own mind he's living in this world or a thousand years ago.'

The eccentric is England's pride, not so much tolerated as admired, their wives a race apart. I said, 'Where is he now?'

'With his boat.' Lucy managed a smile. 'I suppose I

should go and help him. It sounds ridiculous, but he needs me.'

'To build a funeral ship?'

Lucy said, 'I know a woman whose husband makes models of ships out of used matches. It's his hobby. Saul happens to be making a full-sized model of an ancient ship. I don't see what makes it so different.'

I said brutally, 'If you had any sense you'd stop playing the little helpmeet and see if you couldn't get that husband of yours interested in stamp collecting.'

'Please,' Lucy said. 'We were happy till you came.' Those oft-quoted words of reproach, untrue as always. We looked at each other, both full of self-justification.

Laurie stood up, which I knew meant that she had decided we should go, a sensible enough thing in the circumstances. As I stood up too I said, 'Look, the whole thing's best written off as an accident. Your father was in the plane when Smith crashed, full stop. Nobody's going to make inquiries into Smith, it would be too damned embarrassing. What this government doesn't need just now is a news story about how easy it is for private individuals in Britain to get hold of a few tons of bombs and then load them on a plane bound for Dublin.'

Lucy looked at me. 'Promise?'

'No,' I said. 'I can't promise. But I'll do my best.'

Laurie tugged at my arm and as we went out of the door I glanced back and saw that Lucy had got up too and I felt a small spurt of anger. Why did women do these things? I'd have gone back but the tug on my sleeve was insistent. I said, 'She's just lost her father. She doesn't have to go and help that idiot build his bloody boat.'

'Not your business, lover. Leave it be.'

We went out into the early dark. The sky was green where it met the edge of the land and the hungry bats were doing aerobatics between the house and the trees. The air smelled damp and spiked with the first chill of the fall of the year. We walked back to the barn. As we went indoors Laurie said, 'You never said how you knew who Barney was.'

'A lot of little things, I suppose.' It usually was, of course. You're dead lucky if you get things handed to you on a plate. 'I wondered a bit that first day, when those Germans were in the pub. They were pleasant enough, but I noticed Barney got someone else to serve them. His dislike oozed out of him and I wondered why. Also I got the feeling that he was listening to what they were saying—that he understood German. It seemed an odd accomplishment for a simple Lincolnshire pub keeper. Not outrageously so, but unusual.'

'And?'

'He always kept his sleeves rolled down.' Some things sounded ridiculous when you put them into words. I remembered that day when I'd surprised him in the washroom, the way it had reminded me of a woman I'd once questioned who had the same shyness. I said, 'He'd got a camp number tattooed on his arm. And the year he arrived in Wendal coincided with the year James Bazil came back to this country from a prison camp in Russia.' It sounded so thin, and yet it wasn't. It all added up. I said, 'I don't think I really knew until I saw him pull himself up into the bay of that B-24. It's a knack, and I should imagine a damn tricky one to master, but he hadn't forgotten it.'

Later we lay in bed and looked at the first stars through the window, listening to the night sounds, not many in those parts. But the same restless bird that had wittered on previous nights was there on cue. What the devil was it? I waited for Lucy's wolfhound to make his usual response, the huge brute seemed to be as irritated as I was by that unnatural bird, his bay of fury almost shaking the house. God knows how the Haywards slept through it. But no bark this night.

Laurie must have been thinking the same thing, because

she said, 'The dog did nothing in the night. That was the remarkable thing.'

'I never can remember in which story Holmes said that.' I waited for her to tell me, but she didn't and the quote was a bit iffy, anyway. Finally she said, 'You don't suppose Saul's been burgled, do you?'

I rolled over and looked at her, a pleasant enough sight with her shoulders honey against the white of the pillows, tousled a bit in the big bed littered with the hasty cast-offs of reconciliation. I said, 'Why should he be?' I was not much of a policeman at that moment.

'I don't know. Aren't burglars supposed to drug guard dogs before they break in? And Lucy was saying today that all those old swords and things they had on the walls had gone.'

'Odd things to have taken.' The dog. The swords. Had it not been a wolfhound I'd probably still have missed the point, but this was the old hunting dog of the early Brits. It was the kind of dog Saul's ancient forebears would have owned. I swung my legs out of bed and grabbed for my trousers.

'Angus, what on earth . . .'

'Ship burial.' I was on my knees, cursing, grovelling for a lost shoe. 'Ship burial! You were sent off with what you were going to need on the other side. Your weapons, your hunting dogs . . .'

Laurie sat up straight. 'Oh no . . .'

'Oh yes.' I'd found the shoe and dragged it on. 'And their women. Usually a slave girl or two who were supposed to volunteer for the job. There used to be an old woman called "The Angel of Death" who stabbed them before they were dumped on board. But there don't seem to be many slave women around.'

'Angus! Wait!'

But I didn't wait. I was scared out of my mind. I went down the stairs and across the farmyard in a rush before I even registered the fact that I hadn't got around to putting a shirt on and it was cold. I ran past the house and out into the field to where Saul had his ship bunker. It was dark, but not so dark that I couldn't see it against the weird light of the sky. The hump of raised earth and the shadowed entrance of ancient sandbags. I stumbled towards it, guided by the few shafts of light that showed from the bottom of the flight of steps. The door at the bottom was half open and I kicked it aside.

> Then was a mighty pyre prepared
> From which hung helmets and shields and polished
>   armour
> In the manner ordered by the dead hero.
> Upon this the men of battle laid their beloved
>   leader . . .

I could hear Saul's voice chanting from somewhere around the great prow. How the hell did one get to him? I ran along the length of the boat, the swell of its hull above my head. About midships there was a stepladder and I went up it like a window-cleaner. As I reached the top and jumped down to the deck I nearly fell over a dark grey hairy mass. Beowulf. His throat was cut and he oozed blood dark over the scrubbed boards.

> Then the Geats raised a mighty barrow on the cliffs
> High and wide, so that seamen might see it from
>   afar . . .

Saul was standing in the middle of the enormously wide deck. He'd built a great pyre of logs and willow withers, and on top of it was Lucy, with her wrists and ankles bound. Saul was standing over her, the great iron sword of Morcar the Left-Handed clasped in both hands.

> Then a young virgin
> Her hair braided in seemly fashion
> Sang a lament . . .

I said, 'Saul!'

He stopped and stared at me, letting the point of the sword fall to the ground. I think if he'd been wearing a winged helmet and a wolfskin jacket I'd have either laughed or just stood there while he hacked his unfortunate wife's head off. Horror and the ludicrous are often so near they almost touch, and a prosperous farmer dressed like one of King Harold's house kerls would have been hard to take. But Saul Hayward in an old houndstooth jacket waving a sword was just a deranged man about to do someone an injury.

He was looking at me. At least he was staring in my direction. God knows whether he saw me or not, his eyes had the curiously hurt look that seems to belong to a certain type of the insane. If I'd been armed I think I should have risked getting a shot off; as it was I was empty-handed and half a dozen strides away. If I'd a grasp of conversational Anglo-Saxon I might have tried ordering him about in that language, even though the chances were it would have simply pushed him even deeper into the fuzzy fantasy world that was taking over his mind. The silence couldn't go on for ever. When he broke it his voice was thick and husky but oddly chatty.

'It's all right, you know, I'm just taking her with me.' I didn't say anything and he went on, 'Not like the man Whitton. Different thing altogether. It was time the Fen had an offering. Hadn't had one for years and years, so I held him under till the Fen took him and you saw what happened. It gave me back Morcar's burial ship.' He paused. 'It was a sign, of course. That they're waiting for me.'

We looked at each other, then I heard my own voice saying with the air of a competent secretary, 'You're wanted on the telephone. They say it's urgent.'

I watched his eyes and they did change. The hurt look went, to be replaced by one of mild irritation. He lowered the sword carefully and laid it down. He didn't seem to see Lucy, but as he straightened up he said peevishly, 'At this time of night? Who is it?' One could almost hear his mind clicking back into the twentieth century.

'I don't know,' I told him. 'They didn't say.'

I motioned him towards the steps and he went down them obediently and we walked together back to the house. I was sorry having to leave Lucy but I wasn't going to let Saul out of my sight. All the way back across the farmyard he muttered and grumbled to himself, while I hoped against hope that I was right and that his little office hadn't got a window. He was a big man and I'd been bounced about enough already for one night.

'Whoever it is, he'd better make it short,' Saul said. So that he could go back and finish his wife off? Did he actually know what he was doing half the time?

'I'm sure they will,' I said. I hung behind as we went into the office. It was all right, there was no window. I don't think he'd even noticed that the telephone was still in its cradle before I'd got the key out and skipped back into the hall, slamming the door behind me. As I scrabbled to get the key back in my side of the door and turn it, it must have looked like something out of a funny film. But it wasn't funny, it was bloody terrifying. Saul's bellow of rage and the crash of his body on the door gave me a nasty moment, but the door wouldn't have been out of place in a castle.

I left the poor devil to it and went in search of an extension telephone. There was one in the kitchen and I dialled Emergency.

The girl answered instantly. 'Which service do you require?'

'I want a doctor and an ambulance,' I said.

The old airfield looked empty in the early morning light. Before long there would be a lot of gear arriving from the CVA in order to haul what was left of *Liberty Belle* from the fen. They'd have to come because the book of rules said so, but I was rather glad that there wouldn't be anything left to investigate. The living are depressingly ungenerous to anyone who has been careless enough to die an untidy death, and if the authorities had their way they'd fish out what was left of Smith and Barney and clean it up and photograph it and have proper post-mortem examinations to make it official that they'd died in an air crash rather than of bubonic plague. Well, they'd be unlucky this time.

I'd stopped the car at the crossroads beyond the farm so that we could look back at the place. We could see the house and the hangar and the grey strip of runway showing straight among the crops. We seemed to have been there for ever.

Laurie said, 'What will happen to Saul?'

Saul, in hospital by now, being observed, poor devil, while he skated precariously between one millennium and the next. 'He's probably curable,' I said. I didn't know, but they were clever about such things. 'He'll get treatment and he'll go back to Lucy and she'll take care of him. Let's face it, it doesn't matter all that much if he does think he's a Saxon thane half the time so long as they can keep his mind off ritual burials.'

'And murder.'

'The coroner has already decided that Whitton was drowned accidentally, and we can't prove Saul chucked him in the fen as a gift to the gods. Anyway, it won't bring the chap back.'

'I'll be glad to be shot of this place.'

I said, 'Yes.' Beside me, Laurie shivered as though a cold breeze had blown through the car. She hadn't mentioned Smith. Had there been something between the two of them? Or was it just something I'd imagined? I could have asked, but cowardice or caution told me to leave it be. I thought of Lois in Cambridge and unthought her. I said, 'It's been a funny old time.'

I was remembering the local legend of the unidentified Liberator that was supposed to have crashed into the fen during the war. I never had managed to confirm that it had never happened, yet, curiously, it had happened now. I wondered fancifully if the present had at last caught up with the past. Then I stopped wondering as Laurie said, 'What about Segal's death? Will you have to give evidence or anything?'

I said, 'The Coroner will have to hear Lucy's evidence about Barney. Whether he accepts it or not is up to him. It shouldn't be difficult to establish that Barney Sutton and James Bazil were one and the same person, but not much beyond that. There may be a motive for murder and an opportunity, but this late in the day proof is something else again.'

Laurie turned her head and looked at me. 'It'll be good to get back home.'

'Yes.' There's a lot to be said for being a member of a reticent race, and I suppose she was thinking much the same thing, because she laughed.

'Let's be going.'

I prodded the starter and the Maserati growled into life. Smith and his boys had done a nice job on the gear shift. We rolled up to the crossroads and turned right for Peterborough. The road was clear in front of us and we didn't look back.

THE END